GLADIATOR ISLAND

ISLAND

The Creatures

COREY O'NEILL

E

EPIC
Press

The Creatures
Gladiator Island: Book #3

Written by Corey O'Neill

Copyright © 2017 by Abdo Consulting Group, Inc.

Published by EPIC Press™
PO Box 398166
Minneapolis, MN 55439

Cover design by Laura Mitchell
Images for cover art obtained from iStockPhoto.com
Edited by Leah Jenness

LIBRARY OF CONGRESS CATALOGING-IN-PUBLICATION DATA

Names: O'Neill, Corey, author.
Title: The creatures / by Corey O'Neill.
Description: Minneapolis, MN : EPIC Press, [2017] | Series: Gladiator Island ; book #3
Summary: Raised on the island, Chelsea must determine whose side she's on, and whether to
    join a group planning a daring revolt. As Chelsea tries to decipher who is telling the truth,
    she learns some of the islands biggest and most frightening secrets.
Identifiers: LCCN 2015959399 | ISBN 9781680762693 (lib. bdg.) |
    ISBN 9781680762907 (ebook)
Subjects: LCSH: Adventure and adventurers—Fiction. | Interpersonal relationships—Fiction. |
    Survival—Fiction. | Human behavior—Fiction. | Young adult fiction.
Classification: DDC [Fic]—dc23
LC record available at http://lccn.loc.gov/2015959399

EPIC
Press

EPICPRESS.COM

For Dane,
always quick with a kiss

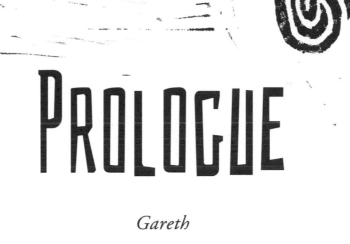

PROLOGUE

Gareth

"Bertram, Bertram, Bertram, it's good to see you my friend."

He stared at me wide-eyed and broke out into a huge grin.

"I thought you were dead . . . so this is sort of like seeing a ghost," Bertram said, reaching over his hand. "It's surreal. It's really you, isn't it? I've missed you very much, Gareth."

I smiled back, took his hand, and pulled him in for a long embrace. He hugged me back and I put my mouth right up to his ear, whispering so the boy next to him couldn't hear me. "I could kill you for bringing the kid. That was the one rule, wasn't it?"

I pulled away and stared him in his eyes. Bertram glanced away and looked down at the boy.

"What was I supposed to do?"

"If I didn't need your help, I'd send you back on the boat right now," I replied, completely unamused at this development.

"He'll stay out of trouble, I promise. Right, Odin?"

The boy looked up at me with big eyes but didn't say anything. I gathered he was around Chelsea's age, or possibly just a year or two older.

"Okay, okay. Odin—is it? Why don't you go on ahead for a second?" I said, and nudged the boy down the dock toward the beach.

When he was out of earshot, I turned to Bertram.

"So, what's this all about?" Bertram asked, gesturing toward the island, his brow furrowed in confusion. "I thought you were dead—what is this place?"

"I'll explain everything once you've settled in, but the long and short of it is that I need your help developing security technology and failsafe programs for a very special project that I've been working on."

"Okay, well, I can certainly help with that . . . but what is the project?" he asked.

"You'll see exactly what I've been developing soon enough, but let's just say I need as much help with keeping things in as with keeping things out . . . "

"That certainly sounds intriguing," Bertram said. I think it was finally dawning on him that this is what I'd been working on all these years, and his confusion turned to giddiness. He slapped me on the back, still in disbelief.

"Do you think you're up for the challenge?" I asked.

"For you, Gareth, I'd do anything. You saved my life."

CHAPTER 1

Chelsea

"You can still join our side, Chelsea. I know you are different from your dad—I see the good in you. And we can get out of here . . . together . . . " Reed said, glaring back at me from a few feet away.

I smirked. Reed had no idea what he was talking about.

I held the dagger up to look threatening, but my arm shook like crazy. It was impossible to get off this island. So many people had tried, but no one had succeeded. He glanced over his shoulder down the hill.

Over and over in my mind, I had replayed Reed plunging the knife into Odin until I made myself sick. This wasn't happening the way we had planned. I was supposed to be on a boat starting a new life with Odin, but here I was instead, trapped on an island with a dead boyfriend, his killer, and a demented father.

My fury toward Reed was so overwhelming, if I could kill him right then and there, I think I'd do it. It was a crazy thought and I'd never taken anyone's life before, but standing there, I felt nothing at all except a debilitating anger toward Reed that soon turned to helplessness. I knew that I didn't stand a chance trying to fight him. Given his recent daily training with Ames, he could take me out if he wanted to. But, instead of lunging toward me, wrestling me to the ground, and strangling me, he looked at me with what seemed to be pity. This made me even angrier.

Reed persisted. "You can still escape, Chelsea. You can leave this all behind."

I shook my head. It wasn't possible, and when I pressed to learn more, Reed was speechless.

I started laughing. They didn't have a real plan. I knew it.

"No one gets out of here alive, Reed. No one. Many have tried, so whatever you're thinking, I doubt you're smarter than everyone else that's attempted to escape and been killed," I said. "Besides, where are you going to go?" I asked.

"I'll go home."

"That's hilarious, Reed. Your parents think you're dead. They've already had your funeral. You have a gravestone already, right next to your drowned brother."

I couldn't help myself, being cruel. I knew it was the meanest thing I could say in the moment, and I twisted my lips into a smile, feeling satisfied with myself.

"What do you mean?" Reed asked.

"Yeah, my dad showed me the article online. He thought it was funny," I said, watching his face go white. "Your boat went down in the ocean. They found the wreckage, but no survivors."

"Why are you saying this to me?" Reed asked.

"You caused me the greatest pain I could ever imagine, taking Odin away from me. Now I am going to do the same."

"So, you are just like your dad?"

I scoffed. How dare he compare me to him? We weren't similar—I was just heartbroken and furious at Reed for taking away the one good thing I had in my life.

"I'm not like him at all, but I'm going to avenge Odin's death," I said, feeling desperate to not let Reed go without punishment.

"Then you're going to have to stop me," Reed said. He suddenly jumped up and ran away from me, down the fence line of the game area toward the thick line of trees that led to the water.

"Stop, Reed!" I screamed.

I started to run after him and tripped, the dagger flying out of my hand into the bushes.

I tried to scramble up and he was nearly out of sight. He turned back to look at me one more time and I yelled to him. "Fucking asshole! I'm going to get you, Reed!"

As he darted into the trees, I called out, hoping he could still hear me as I screamed, "I'm going to make sure you pay for killing Odin! If he couldn't get off the island alive, neither will you!"

I took a deep breath to try to compose myself. I looked down and brushed the dirt and leaves from my nightgown. Why was I chasing after him? His fate was sealed regardless. He was screwed.

I knew there was nowhere Reed could escape to once he got down the hill to the beach. It was kind of funny, actually, thinking about him running until he reached the shore and looking out at the water, realizing there was no place to go except back into the forest and toward my dad's compound.

Trying to hide on the island was impossible unless you knew the secret crannies and passageways that took me my whole life to discover. It was only a matter of time until Reed was either dragged back by Suits or crawled back on his own, hungry, cold, and exhausted.

He'd be back in my dad's control soon enough and would be taken care of. My dad didn't tolerate people who tried to cheat his system. I almost felt sorry for what Reed would face upon his return, as my dad would surely be embarrassed that his prized prisoner had temporarily escaped, and would exact an especially gruesome torture. But then I thought about Odin again, and that pity was pushed aside and all the space in my heart was crammed tight with dark thoughts of revenge.

I needed to talk to my dad to see if he'd finally make good on his promise to me to let me leave of my own free will. It was always *later, later*, but now it was time. I wouldn't wait another day.

Without Odin, I had nothing on the island to live for anymore.

I regretted my recent fight with Odin, over something so stupid and petty that it eventually became about the fight and who was more stubborn. Because I was angry, I taunted Odin by flirting with Reed. Reed was the most obvious choice—good looking, a promising fighter, and someone who caught my dad's interest. My dad never cared for Odin, and the feeling was mutual. So, when Odin and I were in a fight, I shamelessly flirted with Reed right under Odin's nose, humiliating him in front of the others. We eventually made up, as we always did, but looking back now, I hated my actions just the same. The quarrel was the beginning of the end.

After Reed disappeared down to the beach, I turned back and started running up the path to find my dad.

As I got to the top of the mountain and started back down the other side toward the compound,

I spotted Elise standing with Ames close to the building's entrance. They were whispering to each other and Ames looked agitated.

I felt hatred toward them too. They had sided with Reed, partnering with him to try to plot an escape. I was never included in those plans. Suits inferred that since Gareth was my dad, I couldn't be trusted fully. But I wanted to leave just as badly as they did.

As I approached them, they looked over and abruptly went quiet.

I didn't let on that I'd just been with Reed. They understood this island's secret corners just as well as me, and if they knew he was out there by the beach, they'd surely help to keep him hidden away just a while longer.

"Hello there," I said, nodding at them with a smile, and trying not to betray how furious I felt. Elise had once been my closest ally aside from Odin, and she knew how much he meant to me.

She used to say she'd help us escape, but didn't act quickly enough.

When Reed killed him, Odin was just one win away from getting a pass off the island. My dad had promised me that and knowing that Odin and I had a chance to have a life beyond the island gave me just a sliver of hope, even though we had our doubts that my dad was being honest. He disliked Odin and we feared he might change his mind—or worse, kill Odin outright—if Odin got to the sacred ten wins.

Before he died, Odin and I talked many times about how if we were able to escape this place, I'd leave with him. We dreamt about where we'd go and what we'd do. We wanted to head to a city, somewhere with millions of people, and we'd adopt new identities and eat in cafés and explore parks and ride in taxis and be normal people, among normal people, for the first time in our lives.

I glared at Elise.

"What are you doing out here . . . and so early?" Elise asked, looking at me with that suspicious gaze she often wore when she thought I was up to no good.

"I couldn't sleep so I decided to go for a walk up the mountain to see the sunrise," I said, as this was something they knew I did from time to time. Before Odin was made a prisoner, he often joined me too. It was one of our favorite activities. Those were happy memories.

After he was imprisoned, he turned angrier by the day. I was desperate to escape the island to get the old Odin back—the one I'd fallen in love with.

Elise looked me up and down.

"Well, you should get back inside and put on more clothing. You'll catch a cold wearing that," she said, gazing at me slowly and with disapproval.

I glanced down at my nightgown and shrugged. "I'm fine."

Elise didn't like when I wore clothing that

showed too much skin. I knew she didn't approve of the way the Praeclarus men looked at me, like something appetizing that was dangling just out of reach. Secretly, I think she was jealous of their attention since she often whined about being a lonely old maid.

I'd seen old pictures of Elise in her living quarters. They were in dusty frames up on the shelf next to scientific journals and medical textbooks. She was once quite beautiful, with olive skin and pale green eyes. In one photo, she was sitting on the beach with my dad, when he was much younger, her head on his shoulder, and they were both smiling at the camera.

I wondered where the pictures came from—and what their relationship had been like back then. I think the only reason dad still tolerated Elise was that she was the most skilled doctor on the island and the most competent surgeon—and that if he ever got injured or sick, he'd want her to be available to keep him alive.

Whenever I tried to ask Elise about what their relationship had been like, the most I got was that they used to date way back when, but both moved on long, long ago. My dad told me that Elise was just jealous that he got together with my mother after they broke up.

Whenever I wanted a woman to talk to growing up, I longed for my mom, who passed away from illness when I was a very young child. I don't remember her clearly, just that we used to go to the beach to explore and wade together in the shallow water. I couldn't see her clearly in my mind, no matter how much I tried to conjure it. My dad tells me I get my looks from her.

The story goes that when she became sick, she was put in Elise's care, but it was too late and she died shortly after. When I was having dark thoughts, I wondered to myself if maybe Elise didn't try hard enough to save her.

Chapter 2

Elise and Ames seemed annoyed that I was standing there, obviously interrupting their conversation.

"What's wrong with you?" I asked Ames, who was looking around nervously. He wouldn't meet my stare directly.

"Nothing at all. Perfectly fine."

"Chelsea," Elise suddenly interjected. "We are worried about you, after what happened with Odin," she said, reaching over and squeezing my arm. I feigned a smile and tried to ignore the instinct to pull away violently.

"How are you feeling?" she asked.

"Terrible," I spat back.

"I imagine you're angry at Reed," she continued and I felt my body tense up.

"In your heart, you know that anger is misplaced, right? Gareth is to blame here. Think about it."

I didn't want to talk about it with her. "I need to go," I replied, anxious to go find my dad. I had to confront him about everything and demand he finally take action. I couldn't be ignored any longer.

"Things can be different, Chelsea," Elise said, and I could tell she was trying to pull me to their side.

Ames glanced at her with an annoyed expression. I knew he didn't trust me—and maybe he shouldn't, honestly. I wasn't certain who I should align with any longer. My dad had the means to get me off the island, and Elise and Ames had the will.

"It's too late, Elise," I said as I started to push past them to enter the compound. "You didn't do enough for me or for Odin," I spat out, unable to keep myself from placing blame on her. I was angry that they didn't enact the plan to revolt sooner, before Odin was killed.

I felt tears brimming in my eyes and I was pissed at myself for letting them see me cry. I walked as fast as I could for the door and punched in the entrance code quickly. The door slid open and I rushed in. It quickly shut behind me, leaving Elise and Ames standing there together. I had nothing more to say to them.

I wondered if they knew that Reed was missing and if they were out there together to go find him.

Then, I wondered how many of the White Suits were in on Ames's and Elise's plan for a revolt, and whom I could trust. I had to be careful who I spoke to now, and what I shared.

Maybe my own movements were being tracked and reported back to Elise and Ames . . . and that everyone would assume I'm on my dad's side and try to capture me, or worse, kill me, when the fighting started.

I walked quickly down the long hallways—hallways I'd roamed thousands of times over the course of my life. I could practically run through them with my eyes closed.

I passed a White Suit named Jericho, and tried to look normal, quickly wiping away the tears that were falling down my cheeks.

"Chelsea! Are you okay? What are you doing out here, and so early?" he asked, his eyes big and his mouth open. He was always so dumb.

"Oh, just going for a walk."

I tried to sound nonchalant and happy, but the tremble in my voice surely gave me away. "Anyway, I have to go," I said, and moved past him. I quickly looked back and he was staring at me with a puzzled frown, and then he spun around and hurried down the hall.

I wondered whose side he was on. Was he going to find Ames and Elise and let them know where I was heading? I didn't have time to worry about it and continued on at an even faster pace.

As I turned a corner to reach the corridor that led to my dad's private quarters, someone suddenly lunged out of a doorway and grabbed me, toppling me to the ground.

"Ahhhhh. What the hell?" I screamed as I fell, my head hitting the cement, hard. I couldn't see my attacker's face clearly as I was pulled into a darkened room, the door slamming behind us.

I swung my arms at the person on top of me. I tried to punch and kick my way out, but I was overpowered. I feared I was about to get raped or killed, and I screamed out as loud as I could. The person's hand slapped hard over my mouth, silencing me.

I bit it hard and felt blood on my lips.

"Fuck! What are you doing?!" the person screamed out and I immediately recognized the voice. Ames. When he got off of me, I stood up and lunged at the door, pulling it hard, but it wouldn't budge.

I punched in the code, which didn't work either. "What the hell?" I spat out, flipping on the light switch. I turned around to face Ames.

"What do you think you're doing?" I asked.

"We're not letting you go talk to Gareth, that's what," he said.

I backed away from him, terrified, and then darted toward the door again.

"Don't worry, I'm not going to hurt you, if that's what you're scared about. I'm not some monster, Chelsea, like your dad."

I felt a moment of relief, which was quickly replaced by anger.

"You can't stop me from talking to him," I spat at him, turning to input the code again, then yanking at the door, which didn't budge.

"What did you do?" I asked and turned to look at him, surprised that the code that I had typed in thousands of times wasn't working anymore.

"We're smarter and more capable than you may realize, and it's time we get off this island," he said. He was sweaty and his eyes were practically bugging out of his skull.

"That's impossible," I said.

"No, it's actually very possible, and you have a choice now."

I looked at him, trying to figure out how I could get past him. He had been a special operations fighter and martial arts master before coming to the island, so if challenging Reed was a bad idea, the thought of going up against Ames was laughable.

He raised his eyebrows, smirking, as if reading my mind.

"So, it's time to decide whose side you're on. Are you going to join us?"

CHAPTER 3

Chelsea — Age 9

That day years ago when Odin first arrived, I was incredibly bored. I wanted to draw a map of the island that was right, with trees and benches and paths in their correct place. I'd spent days drawing sketches of the birds I saw in the trees, the shells on the beach, and even the pebbles that lined the path up the mountain, but I was feeling tired and up for a new adventure.

I had no one to talk to except Elise and my dad, but they didn't like to play with me and they were always distracted by work or friends.

All my dad cared about was hanging out with his weird, snobby friends that came to the island every couple of months to go hunting and do other stuff that didn't make much sense to me. They were friendly and I liked the gifts they brought, but they made me feel weird when they doted on me too much.

When his friends weren't visiting, my dad was obsessed with how to make the island even better, whatever that meant. To me, that seemed crazy, because the island already had a lot of stuff for adults to do. It's all he talked about. I bugged him that he needed to add more things for me to entertain myself—stuff for kids—but he never listened to me.

My dad and his friends started out hunting deer in the game area, but that soon became too easy, according to him, and he worried that the island was growing dull. So then he brought in bears, and then he shipped in lions and tigers, and even elephants. I loved seeing the creatures up

close, but I felt bad for them being cooped up in the game area. It was a large enclosure with lots of shrubbery and rocks and trees, but they were still caged. The animals looked to me like they were meant to roam free.

When I asked my dad where he got the animals from, he laughed and told me "the zoo." Elise just shrugged when I asked her, like she wanted no part of it.

During that time, new people started arriving on the island by boat—young men and women that became the staff. The pretty ones got to live in nice living quarters and go wherever they wanted, for the most part. I watched them hang out with the visitors whenever they arrived and make them laugh and stuff.

The other ones wore all white. They kept the island clean, cooked everyone's food, planted the gardens, and eventually built the new buildings and the Coliseum. They were all very friendly to me, and I liked them, but they weren't my age and couldn't play with me.

I wanted someone to explore with—to go swimming in the ocean with on warm days and to hike up the mountain with to look for fairies and elves in the forested hills. I longed for someone my own age to play checkers with and to sing silly songs with and to make gigantic sand castles on the beach with. Elise played with me sometimes, but it wasn't the same. I read about friends in books and I wanted to feel friendship with another kid.

So, as I set out up the mountain on the island to try to draw out every path and building and tree, I thought about how wonderful it would be to have someone by my side for adventures.

As I got to the top of the mountain, I looked around at the view of the ocean on all sides and the greenery and the buildings. This was my favorite place and I couldn't help but smile. Everything looked small, like a doll's version of the island. I saw in the distance a boat arriving at the dock and I wondered who it could be.

The only boats that came by were invited visitors or new staff, and no one had mentioned to me that we were expecting new people. Instead of starting my drawing, I stopped to watch. It took a long time and even though it was boring staring at that boat moving so slowly until it reached the dock's side, something told me to wait and watch it. I sat there not moving for what felt like forever. I pulled out my pocket binoculars so I could get a better look.

Finally, a few White Suits appeared, walking very quickly down the dock, and they tied up the boat. Then they stood still, waiting.

A man stepped off the boat and then turned back to the ship, extending his hand. A boy grabbed it and jumped onto the dock, stretching out his arms and looking around. I felt my heart beat like crazy. It was another kid. He appeared to be about my age, but I couldn't be sure, given the squinty view I had through the binoculars and not ever seeing a boy my age before.

Who was he, and why was he here with that man? Had my dad brought me a friend?

I had mentioned my loneliness many times and usually he seemed not to care much about it, or just gave me new presents of toys and candies and pet animals to try to make me feel better.

Yes, that must be it. My dad loved me and wanted to make me happy. I abandoned my plan to draw a map and ran as fast as I could back down the path to find my dad and thank him, and hopefully meet the boy. I skipped past White Suits and other staff members, smiling and laughing when they asked where I was going, and I just kept running until I rushed into my dad's quarters.

He was putting on a jacket and seemed surprised to see me burst into his room.

"Who is he, Dad?" I asked excitedly as I rushed in to give him a hug. He looked down at me, surprised, but hugged me back regardless and sort of laughed.

"What do you mean?"

"The boy! The boy who just arrived on the dock with the man. Who is he?"

"I'm afraid I don't know what you're talking about," my dad said, looking troubled.

"Hahaha funny . . . you finally brought me a playmate, didn't you? Thank you so much, Dad! I'm so, so excited . . . can we go meet him?"

My dad pulled away from me and muttered, "God dammit, Bertram."

"What?"

"You stay right here, Chelsea. Do not leave this room, you understand me?" my dad said, glaring at me. I knew he was serious. He rushed out, not even bothering to comb his hair.

"Yes, sir," I said, backing down a little bit and feeling confused. I wanted to go meet the boy right away.

After my dad left, I wondered what to do next.

I could follow him and go try to spy on what he was doing, but if he caught me, I'd be in trouble and probably locked in my room for a week, which was the worst and most boring punishment ever.

Or, I could sit here, as he ordered, and wait and hope for the best. I looked around the room. I rarely got time in here alone, and I wondered if I could uncover any secrets.

I turned and stared at the ceiling and corners of the room. There were two cameras pointing inward—one toward the sitting area and desk, and the other at the bedroom. As long as I appeared like I wasn't getting into any trouble, I'd be fine looking around a little bit. I thought I spotted my dad's notebook on the desk. He had never let me see what was scribbled inside, and always snapped it shut when I tried to sneak a look.

I wondered how I could read it and quickly came up with a plan.

I walked over to the tall, long bookshelf and

scanned all the titles, finally pulling out a large, heavy book from a low shelf. It had a picture of seaweed and fish on the cover with the title, *Biological Diversity of the Indian Ocean Islands,* in big black print. I didn't know what that meant exactly, but that didn't matter to me.

I went over to my dad's desk, sat down in the giant leather chair, and saw that indeed the book I had glanced out of the corner of my eye was my dad's prized notebook. He must've forgotten it in his haste to leave the room.

I put down the Indian Ocean book and opened it, glancing up at the position of the security camera. From there, I was pretty sure it couldn't see exactly what I was looking at, so I put the ocean book on top of the notebook, and then slid the notebook from under the book toward me until I could clearly see the pages.

It was open to March fourteenth and there was a note in big red letters: *Bertram Securities, 10:00 am.*

I didn't know what that meant except that it had to do with the man who had arrived with the boy. *What does "Bertram" mean?* I asked myself.

I flipped through the other pages and saw fancy drawings of buildings and codes that I didn't understand. There were also funny pictures of animals that looked like the monsters I saw in my two prized Greek mythology books—tigers crossed with alligators, and lions with eagle heads. I knew my dad was a good artist, as he used to share little doodles with me when I was feeling sad, but I hadn't seen these drawings before. They were peculiar and I wondered if my dad just scribbled them for his own amusement. I was surprised to see such silly illustrations since my dad was always so serious. They made me laugh out loud.

As I was flipping through the notebook trying to make sense of the weird stuff it contained, I heard the door beeping and rushed to turn the notebook back to March fourteenth before sliding it under the Indian Ocean book, which was opened up to a page with a large drawing of a whale.

I looked down at the whale drawing like it was the coolest thing in the world, and smiled wide when my dad entered with a man following behind him, but no boy.

"What are you up to, Chelsea?" my dad asked, and I smiled sweetly.

"Just learning about whales, Dad. They're pretty neat," I said, causing his expression to soften just a little bit. I was good at distracting him from any trouble I might be getting into.

"Chelsea, this is Bertram," he said, gesturing to his side.

The man had red hair and a ruddy face, and he smiled at me kindly and said, "Hi."

"Hello," I responded, not sure what to say next.

"Bertram is one of my oldest, dearest friends, Chelsea. And, after much convincing, he's finally decided to come live with us on the island."

"Bertram is among a handful of people in the

whole world that I trust with my life, and he's here to make us safer," he continued, but I didn't understand what that meant. I didn't feel in danger on the island.

"And what about the boy that I saw?" I asked, looking at both of them, confused.

Bertram was about to speak, when my dad stopped him, quickly darting out his arm and grabbing Bertram's shoulder.

"Chelsea, Bertram and I had a disagreement about this. Watching you, I know this island is no place for a young person to grow up. You've said so yourself—how bored and miserable you are."

I felt my heart sink, as my dad hadn't brought me a friend after all. They were going to ship the boy back to wherever he came from—I just knew it.

My dad continued to speak.

"But, after some convincing, Bertram assured me that his boy would not be any trouble, and suggested he might even be a good playmate for you," my dad said. I looked up, waiting.

"So, even though I was angry at Bertram for disobeying my orders, I know what it's like to be a father, and finally we came to an agreement," he looked over at Bertram, who nodded.

"The boy can stay as long as he doesn't get into any trouble, and that also means you stay out of trouble with him," my dad said, looking at me with his stern stare. But I knew he did this to make me happy and I smiled wide at him.

"Of course, Dad. We will stay out of the way. Thank you!" I exclaimed. Bertram smiled and laughed, and my dad joined in. He then went to the door, opened it, and beckoned someone to come in.

I was excited as I looked at the door, and suddenly, the boy slid through the opening, looking down at his feet.

"Odin, say hello," Bertram prompted. The

boy slowly looked up and stared at me. I felt my cheeks turn hot and I smiled back.

"Hello," I said. He looked back with serious, dark eyes, but finally said hi.

I felt so happy I couldn't help but run over and give my dad a big hug. He lifted me up in the air and swung me around. As I passed Odin, I caught him smiling at me, just a little bit.

CHAPTER 4

I glared up at Ames, furious that he was holding me captive in this room. By the looks of the bed and the shabby furnishings, it was for a prisoner in solitary confinement. I knew my screams wouldn't penetrate the thick walls, no matter how loudly I yelled.

"My dad will kill you for taking me," I spat at him. Ames shrugged.

"Obviously." He paused, and looked at me wryly. "Do you know how long I've known your dad?"

I had no idea, I just knew that when Ames arrived, my dad and him already had a history that went way back, before the island.

"Longer than you've been alive. Longer than the island itself. I'm one of Gareth's only friends, yet I still know he'd kill me without hesitation," he said, looking me up and down. "And Chelsea, he's never, ever letting you off of this island, no matter what he's promised."

I tried to look dismissive, but I wondered if he was speaking the truth.

My dad was aware I had feelings for Odin. He'd known for years and never approved. Despite my pleas, when Odin got in trouble, my dad made him a fighter. When that all happened and I realized what that meant for Odin, I was filled with blind rage and refused to talk to him for weeks. It seemed like all hope was lost.

But then, my dad said that when Odin had ten wins, he'd let both of us leave together and start a new life. He promised me at least that, and I held onto that hope that we'd eventually get to live together somewhere in the world, free.

When I saw what a good fighter Odin was and

realized that his battles might be our ticket off the island, I felt just a tiny bit better and tried to get along with my dad as best I could, as I didn't want him to change his mind. I wanted a chance to live free with Odin more than anything.

Odin and I hatched a plan on how we could ensure he beat Reed, if they were to be matched up. The Praeclarus members liked watching Reed fight, and I worried that my dad might change his mind about the ten win rule and make sure Odin didn't get out of the fight alive. He never liked Odin and he always wanted to give Praeclarus the best fight possible.

After Reed killed Odin, I ran away from the Coliseum to my room and cried and cried and cried until there was nothing left, and I lay on my bed, weak and sick to my stomach. Just as I started to drift off to sleep, my dad entered the room, appearing upset. He sat next to the bed and pet my hair.

"I'm so sorry, Chelsea," he said. When I looked

at him, I thought his eyes were glassy, like he'd been crying. I believed he was telling the truth.

"He was my one true love, Dad," I sobbed. He leaned in, hugged me, and held me close.

"Oh, Chelsea, I am devastated too. I really thought there was no way Reed was going to beat Odin. Odin was so strong, I didn't believe Reed was actually a worthy opponent," he said.

"It's too late. I hate that you made him a fighter . . ." I cried.

"Be careful there . . . let's not get started again. You know why I did that, Chelsea," my dad said. "I always have to protect our safety, above all else. And sometimes the cost of that protection is very grave. I'm worried, you know," he said. I lifted my head to look at him.

"About what?"

"I've heard whispers that people are trying to stage an uprising, but I'm not sure who is at the root or what the plan is. I've asked my closest advisors, and no one is giving me consistent information," he said. "We have to stop it, Chelsea. Remember, if the world finds out about the island, you and I and everyone else here will be killed. Everything I've ever done was to protect both of us."

I was doubtful and continued to cry for a long time. My dad was silent as he rubbed my back.

Finally, he spoke again. "Chelsea, you know that I love you more than anyone else in the entire world?"

"Yes," I spoke quietly as snot ran down my face. I wiped at it with the back of my hand, and my dad handed me a purple handkerchief.

"And, even though my greatest joy in the world is seeing your smiling face, I want more than anything for you to spend the rest of your days happy?"

"Okay."

"I don't want you to be here if anything happens."

"What do you mean?"

"I will create a new identity for you. I will buy you a house or condo or whatever you want in the country of your choosing. I will put millions of dollars into a bank account for you. I will get you a job that excites you—maybe as an artist? Whatever you want."

"But why now?"

"I feel terrible about Odin. I want you to live the life of a young adult with a wide open future ahead of you."

It sounded too good to be true, and I tried to figure out his angle, as he *always* had one.

"But Chelsea, setting this up so that no one finds you out is going to take time for me. I'll work with Praeclarus to do all of this, but you have to give me time," he said, looking at me very seriously.

I nodded.

"And, one other thing . . . even though I know people are trying to stage a revolt, I'm not certain who is involved and when this is all happening.

Someone on my team is lying to me, but I'm not sure who. So, to protect both of us, if you hear of anything . . . anything at all . . . you must come to me right away so I can put a stop to it immediately. That's what I need to ensure we both stay alive, and so I can get you out of here. You understand?"

I paused, thinking hard about what he was telling me.

"Yes," I finally responded, feeling just a tiny bit of hope. I knew it might be misplaced, but I couldn't believe my dad would lie to me again when my own safety was in doubt. If a revolt started, I needed to be on the right side of the fight.

"Be patient with me, Chelsea," he said, squeezing my hand very hard. I winced but nodded. Then he stood up and walked out of the room.

My mind reeled, trying to figure out my next steps.

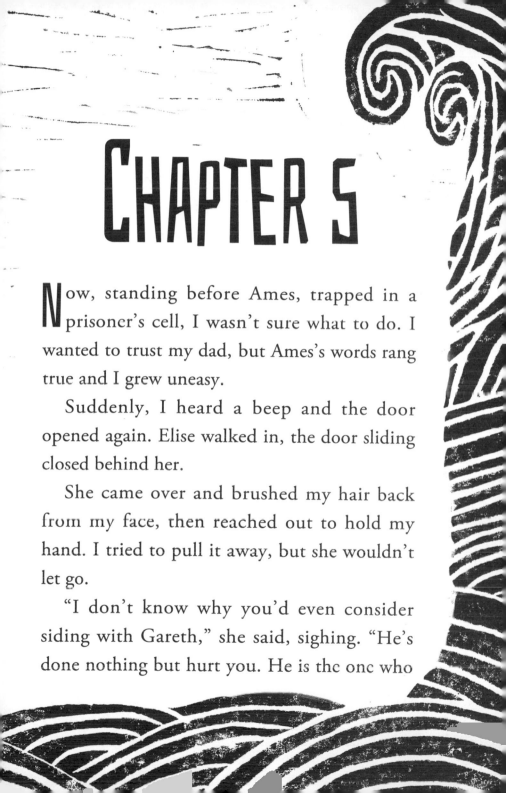

CHAPTER 5

Now, standing before Ames, trapped in a prisoner's cell, I wasn't sure what to do. I wanted to trust my dad, but Ames's words rang true and I grew uneasy.

Suddenly, I heard a beep and the door opened again. Elise walked in, the door sliding closed behind her.

She came over and brushed my hair back from my face, then reached out to hold my hand. I tried to pull it away, but she wouldn't let go.

"I don't know why you'd even consider siding with Gareth," she said, sighing. "He's done nothing but hurt you. He is the one who ordered Odin to be enslaved, and he's the reason Odin is dead today. Reed is not at fault here."

I shook my head, thinking about my dad's promise to help me as the image of Reed stabbing Odin to death played in my mind.

"Anyway, I don't know if it was you that told him," Elise continued, "but Gareth thinks the revolt is starting very soon." She then turned to Ames, "He's ordered a full lockdown of all facilities starting at four p.m. today. Our plan is going to have to wait. I've already sent a Suit to track down Reed, and to bring him back to his quarters ASAP."

Ames sighed heavily. "Again?"

"Yes, but we must be patient, and choose our time of attack wisely. We only have one shot at this. Now, Ames, can you please leave us alone? I need to speak to Chelsea privately."

Ames looked at both of us with raised eyebrows. "Fine," he said, sounding annoyed as he left the room.

When he was gone, Elise looked at me and asked, "What has Gareth promised you?"

I was surprised, but shook my head, confused.

"I don't know what you mean."

"Did he promise to create a new life for you, to buy you a piece of property somewhere, to give you loads of money and the like?"

I was silent, not wanting to respond, and tried to not feel intimidated by her searching my face for a response.

"Ah ha! Just as I thought," she said, nodding her head.

"Fine . . . " I sighed. "How did you know that? Were you eavesdropping into our conversations?"

"No, but Gareth made the same promises to me."

"Okay, well then I'm happy for both of us that he'll get us out of here safely before any violence begins," I replied, trying to shake her off. I didn't want her to poke holes in my need for my dad to be telling the truth.

"No, no, you don't understand. Gareth made that promise to me ten years ago, and look at where I am now," she said, gesturing to our dim surroundings. "He manipulates people, Chelsea. That's what he does best. He holds people close and toys with them, and gets their hopes up," she said, staring into my eyes. "You'll never escape this island unless you join us, Chelsea. I was also patient for a long time, waiting for Gareth to make good on his promises. He said he loved me after all, and wanted me to be happy. But I'm still waiting."

I was confused and angry. I didn't know who to believe.

"Chelsea. I love you. I enjoyed watching you grow up to be such a smart, confident woman and was happy to see you experience romantic love with Odin. But I knew you'd never find true happiness with him unless we got both of you off the island."

"That's what Odin and I were trying to do," I

blurted out. "He was one win away from getting off the island, and I was going to join him," I said, feeling angry once again.

"That was a lie, Chelsea," Elise said, sighing audibly. "Gareth is never, ever going to let anyone but Praeclarus members leave this island alive. There's too much at risk. Think about it rationally. I wish you would just see past that he's your dad and recognize that I'm the one on your side, trying to help you."

I glared back at her, not wanting to believe what she was telling me.

She continued, "We were trying to push the plan through as quickly as possible to save Odin, but couldn't move fast enough and I'm so terribly sorry for that. It will be one of my biggest regrets, not being able to save both of you," she said with tears in her eyes.

I didn't know what to think, but felt more confused than ever.

"So, you're just going to keep me locked up in

here forever? My dad will be looking for me," I said.

"Yes, I know," she replied. "That is why you're going to walk out of here and go on pretending we never had this conversation. When the time is right, I'll come find you and you can join us as we leave this place for good. We have enough support to make this work, but we need to be careful now. Gareth knows something is going on, and we have to catch him off guard. Please, Chelsea, think about what I've said and come with us."

And with that, she opened the door and walked out, letting me walk out freely as well. When I stepped through the doorway, I looked down the hall and she was already gone.

I thought about my next step, and whether I should tell my dad everything, but Elise's words kept repeating in my mind.

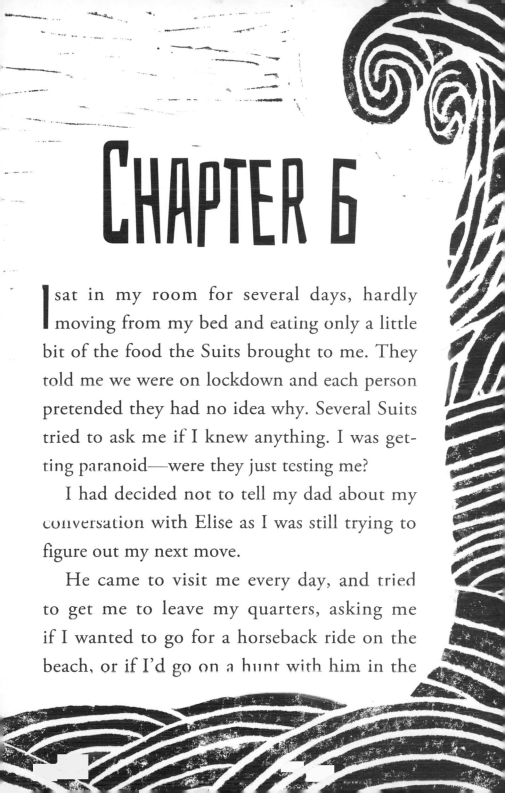

Chapter 6

I sat in my room for several days, hardly moving from my bed and eating only a little bit of the food the Suits brought to me. They told me we were on lockdown and each person pretended they had no idea why. Several Suits tried to ask me if I knew anything. I was getting paranoid—were they just testing me?

I had decided not to tell my dad about my conversation with Elise as I was still trying to figure out my next move.

He came to visit me every day, and tried to get me to leave my quarters, asking me if I wanted to go for a horseback ride on the beach, or if I'd go on a hunt with him in the game area, or watch the boys and girls fight in the training ring. That used to be one of our favorite activities to do together—mostly for me because I got to see Odin.

Now that he was gone, the idea of watching training sessions just made me upset.

"No, I don't want to go watch training," I said and turned away from him, angry and in no mood to talk.

"Remember, Chelsea, I need more time, and I'm going to help you," he said as he pet my hair. I pulled away, not wanting him to touch me. There was a long pause and then he looked at me with a mischievous grin.

"What?" I asked, recognizing that look. He was up to something.

"I think I'm finally ready to show you the airplane hangar."

I was surprised, as I'd asked him about going there nearly every day for many years. It had become a running joke between us, as he always said no. That never stopped me from trying to ask again.

"Really? Are you lying to me?" I asked. I didn't believe him after all of these years.

"Of course not, Chelsea! I just think that what I've been working on is finally ready to be shared—and you're the first person I want to show it to," he explained. He looked at me and smiled so kindly, I believed him and felt a little twinge of hope and excitement. I sat up slowly and wiped the snot from my face with my sleeve

"Lovely," he joked. "Now, get dressed," he ordered and then turned around to look the opposite direction while I got my clothes on.

I'd wondered every day for years about what was in the hangar—the giant building at the end of the island that loomed large in my imagination.

"Let's go," he said after I changed. We set out down the long halls and then headed down the outdoor path toward the restricted area where the hangar was located, behind impossibly tall barbed wire fences and White Suits that never bent to my flirtatious advances.

The walk to the gate took about twenty minutes, and we barely spoke at all. I still was unsure if I could trust him, but I felt just the tiniest bit of excitement. I knew something crazy was in the hangar—it was the only area of the island that I was forbidden from exploring.

We got to the gate and the White Suit named Wexler greeted my dad and looked at me, surprised.

"You're bringing a visitor today? Are you sure it's ready?"

"Yes, it's finally time," my dad said. Wexler nodded and pushed a button for the gate to open for us.

"You need any backup today?" Wexler asked. My dad shook his head.

"No, we'll be just fine," he said as he pushed me forward.

We continued to walk down a very narrow

path, its sides closing in with thick, green shrubbery. I couldn't even see the hangar yet as we took several switchbacks down the hill until finally, the large cement building came into view.

It was huge up close—with high gray walls that reached up way above us. I'd only seen it from very far on top of the mountain, and now, standing next to it, I couldn't believe how big it was. What could possibly be inside of here that needed such a large space?

"It's gigantic, Dad," I said in disbelief, feeling a little giddy with anticipation.

He laughed. "Yes, well it needs to be in order to contain what is inside, and to protect what I've been working on all of these years from prying eyes—like yours," he said, joking with me.

"Now, I don't want you to be scared by what you see inside," he continued. "With years of security planning, we ensured that every precaution was taken to keep us safe, okay?"

I had no idea what he was talking about, but

nodded my head. I knew Bertram had worked on the overall security systems of the island as a whole, so I always felt safe. He had supposedly been one of the top security experts in the world before he came to the island.

My dad took a thin, silver strand tucked underneath his shirt and lifted it over his head, revealing a small key. He then used the key to unlock a box on the wall, next to the front door. He opened the box's door and revealed a different style of keypad than I'd seen before and pressed his thumb against it, causing the whole frame to light up in blue. An alarm sounded loudly before the door slid open.

As it opened, I heard a sharp, guttural shriek come from inside, and then a long howl followed by strange screams of some other creature. I had no idea what kind of animal made those noises, and I jumped back.

The room was still dark and my dad moved inside, reaching back to offer me his hand.

I hesitated, feeling afraid. It suddenly dawned on me. Maybe this was a trap of some sort. Maybe my dad thought I was joining the rebellion and he was taking me to be killed by some animal as punishment. Maybe this was where he had taken Bertram?

"What are you scared of?" my dad asked, looking at me bemused. "Are you afraid of whatever lies within—or of me?"

After he said it, he laughed really, really hard.

I could tell he was testing me. I remembered what Elise said about him being a master manipulator, and I couldn't help but feel he was toying with me just to see how I'd react.

I contemplated turning and running as the sounds of whatever animals were inside grew louder and angrier and more insistent. But I was also curious. I'd been dying to know what was inside this building for years, and I was pretty sure my dad wouldn't hurt me, although I wasn't certain.

"I'm not afraid of you," I insisted, even though my legs were trembling beneath me.

"Good, then take my hand, my dear, and come check this out," he said.

I finally stepped forward and held out my hand. He grabbed it in his firm, warm grip and pulled me forcefully inside. The door snapped shut behind us.

It was pitch black and I couldn't help but lean into him, terribly frightened. The sounds of the animals were unusual and frightening.

"Turn on the lights!" I pleaded, leaning my body against his back, wanting to run away.

My dad shushed me and I repeated my demand again, but he just laughed and didn't do anything. My dad always liked messing with people for fun, and I was fed up.

"Enough already," I demanded, pulling away from him. "Just turn on the lights and show me what all the fuss is about," I insisted.

"Not so fast, love. Just be quiet and listen for a moment," he instructed.

I stood silently, knowing that with my dad, I didn't have much of a choice but to do what he said. The sooner I obeyed, the sooner it would all be over. We stood silently next to each other as I heard animals cry and sniffle and howl and shriek and scream.

"Isn't that beautiful?" Dad asked.

"What?" I was confused.

"These are the sounds of new life," he said, his voice filled with excitement. "It almost makes me want to cry. It's the most amazing thing I've ever heard."

"Okay, yes," I agreed, still not getting it, but knowing the quicker I agreed with whatever he believed, the sooner he'd move on.

"So, are you ready to see something that only a handful of other people in the whole world have experienced?" he asked.

"Umm . . . okay," I said, unsure of what he

could possibly mean. I heard him shuffle back toward the wall and switch on the lights, which blinded my eyes for a moment.

As they adjusted, I saw that we stood at the mouth of a long, impossibly tall room and that the entire corridor was lined with rows of large, metal cages.

We were a good thirty yards away from the nearest row and I couldn't quite make out what was angrily pacing back and forth in the front cage. It didn't look like any animal I'd ever seen, as it was both hairy and scaly, and when it turned to look at us, it appeared to have a long snout, like an alligator.

"What the hell is that?" I asked, stepping back, suddenly feeling very scared.

"Come here," my dad said, ordering me to move closer. "He can't bite from inside his cage."

I took a few tentative steps toward the enclosure, and tried to understand what I was looking at, but my brain couldn't figure out what to make of what it saw.

"That one's not quite ready. Come take a look at this one over here," he said, beckoning me toward a different cage across the hallway.

The animal inside appeared to have the body of a gorilla and the head of a black lion. Instead of a golden mane, its hair was jet black. As we approached, the animal rushed forward and snarled at me, its gigantic sharp teeth gnashing at the cage bars. Instead of lion paws, it had huge, black hands that it beat against the cage, roaring at us angrily.

"What is this?" I asked, horrified as I looked around at the other cages and saw other strange, terrifying animals—or monsters—I wasn't sure what they were, exactly.

"These are my Creatures," my dad said, looking around the room with great admiration. "I've been waiting for the day to show you all this," he continued, stepping close to the animal's cage. He peered at the Creature closely.

"Isn't it beautiful to behold? It has the appetite of a lion—a carnivore—but also has the great intelligence of a gorilla. This guy is very cunning. In developing these Creatures, we tried to take the most compelling characteristics of various animals and melded them together to make Super Creatures, as I like to call them. We even tweaked them to make them more aggressive and easily provoked, when necessary. We don't want sleepy, passive animals . . . right?" he asked, peering at me with a smile. "No, that wouldn't be fun," my dad said, seeming pleased with himself.

It dawned on me that these animals were incarnations of the weird animals I'd seen sketched crudely in my dad's notebook years ago, the day that Odin came to the island.

It seemed impossible, these creatures' very existence.

"This is insane," I blurted out, suddenly feeling scared of my dad. How had he accomplished this?

"This is my life's work, right here," he said. "This is why I built the island in the first place. This is why I charge huge sums to Praeclarus members to come here and enjoy all the illicit things one can't find elsewhere. It's to fund this. And, twenty years later, I'm finally ready to share it with you, and eventually many more people. You know what they'll say, the Praeclarus members, when they see this?" he asked, looking at me with a funny smile.

"No, I have no idea."

"They'll say I just might be a God," he said, laughing, and ignoring the gorilla lion thing behind him as it continued to roar angrily and bash its hands against its caged walls.

CHAPTER 7

The day we met in my dad's study when I was just nine, Odin was painfully shy as we snuck glances at each other. After our introductions, Bertram and my dad led us to the swimming pool with picnic lunches before heading off to go talk about stuff we didn't understand. We sat on the reclining chairs, with me trying to get Odin to talk. I asked him lots of questions he didn't want to answer.

"So, where are you from?"

"How old are you?"

"Have you ever seen a movie in a theater?"

"What's the biggest city you've ever been to?"

"Where is your mom?"

As I pried, he wouldn't even look my way. He lay back on the chair and stared up at the sky, seeming very sad. I so badly wanted to know about the world he left behind.

We sat in silence for a while and I tried to figure out how to get him to come out of his shell.

"Want to see something cool?" I asked, finally breaking the silence as an idea popped into my head. "I promise it's awesome."

He looked over at me and I smiled at him. He kind of smiled back just a tiny bit and my heart raced with excitement.

"Okay, I guess," he said, with an accent that I didn't recognize. He didn't sound like my dad or Elise or any of the visitors to the island. I wondered where he called home before arriving at the island.

I stood up and held out my hand. He reached for it, and I pulled him up and took him toward the path that led to the game reserve. We were

quiet on the walk. I looked over at him sometimes and he looked very serious. He was taller than me and maybe older than me, too, but I couldn't be sure. When he did smile back a little at me, I felt excited in a way that felt weird and good at the same time.

There were no Praeclarus visitors at the island now, so the game area was quiet. As we approached, Odin looked surprised and finally broke his silence.

"What is this place?" he asked, his eyes wide as we walked up to the tall fence. On the other side, a giant brown bear was sprawled out, leaning against the metal, fast asleep.

"Whoa! Is that what I think it is?" he asked. I nodded.

"Come on, I want to show you more—" I said and pulled him forward.

As we walked around the edge, I told him all about Praeclarus, and the fact that I'd been here on the island since I was born. Odin couldn't believe everything I was telling him, and if it wasn't for seeing the tigers and elephants in the flesh, the whole thing might've seemed like a dream that he was waiting to wake up from.

"I love animals," he said, looking sad as we stood in front of the tiger, who paced around its enclosure.

"Back home I have a pet dog that we had to leave behind," he mumbled. It was the most words I'd heard him speak since arriving.

"I'm sorry," I said, feeling bad for him. I knew he wasn't likely to see that dog ever again. I didn't say that though.

"I love animals too. I have a couple of cats, a rabbit, and a parakeet," I said. "They can be your pets too," I offered. It seemed nice, but maybe made him sadder, as he didn't say anything back to me.

"Are you hungry?" I asked him. He nodded yes. I told him to follow me back down the path to the bench that overlooked the whole island and the ocean. We sat down, and I took off my back-pack and unzipped it.

"Check this out," I said, hoping to cheer him up. He leaned over and looked into my bag, which was filled with candy bars and sweet treats from around the world, gifts from Praeclarus men.

When Odin saw what was inside, he laughed out loud and that made me happy.

"Where'd you get all of this?"

"I'm spoiled rotten here and get all sorts of cool stuff," I said, bragging just a little bit. "But, guess what?" I asked, looking at him and smiling.

"What?"

"Since you're my friend, I'll share everything with you," I said, and I meant it.

He was quiet and serious, but I liked him. We opened up a bunch of the candy bars and sat there, taking turns biting into each one and talking about which ones we liked the best.

When we were full and buzzing with sugar, we

both laughed as I told him dumb jokes that were printed in the candy wrappers.

Suddenly, he cut me off mid-giggle and said, "Since you asked, I'm from Ireland and I'm eleven years old."

I'd read about Ireland and that it was very green and magical, and I felt bad that he was taken away from such an amazing place.

"Do you know any leprechauns?" I asked, totally serious, but this just caused him to laugh super hard and tell me no, of course not.

We spent the rest of the day walking around the island and I showed him everything—where my room was, where his room was, the beaches and forests, and where the men in the white suits were starting to build a large coliseum.

"That's amazing," he said as we stared down at the construction. I agreed. It was pretty cool even if I didn't understand why my dad was making it.

When it got dark, we went to the dining hall and met Bertram and my dad, who were deep in conversation about protecting some building, but when they realized we were listening in, my dad changed the subject.

He looked over at both of us and welcomed us to the table. I caught Odin staring up at the stuffed animal heads that lined the tall wall behind my dad. He looked upset.

"Sit down, son," my dad ordered. We sat across from them. As soon as we did, the Suit named Titus came in with a cart of food and placed plates of steaming meat and potatoes in front of us.

"Thank you, sir," my dad said to Titus. "Oh and Titus, we need to talk later tonight about this week's findings," he said. Titus nodded, smiled, and exited the room.

I wondered what that was about.

"I thought this meal would remind you of home," my dad said. Bertram agreed, sounding appreciative.

Since we'd only eaten candy all day, I had a stomachache but managed to take a few bites. I looked over at Odin who was eating everything quickly.

"So, did you two stay out of trouble today?" my dad asked.

"Of course," I assured him and tapped Odin's shin lightly under the table with my toe. He nodded, smiling.

He was my partner in crime now, and I couldn't be more excited to spend the coming days showing him all of the island's coolest places.

"You know how long Bertram and I have known each other?" my dad asked me. Of course I had no idea.

"He helped me start my first company many, many years ago. He was the only person who believed in me, and that was willing to financially support me at the time. I wouldn't be the person I am today, or have the opportunity to create something like this, without Bertram. He was truly the secret to my success," my dad looked over at Bertram warmly, who smiled back.

"And it's time I repay the favor and take care of you both," he continued, looking at Odin. "You'll never be hungry again here, son. I'll give you everything you'll ever need," he said.

I felt like the odd person out in the conversation, like they all shared a secret I didn't understand.

"Well, enough of that serious talk for now," my dad said. "Who's ready for dessert?"

And just like that, Titus suddenly appeared again, this time with my very favorite treat, something called a Baked Alaska that we only had on particularly special occasions. He appeared with the flaming dessert and set it carefully in front of us. The flame died out and we all clapped.

My dad let me slice into the meringue and give each person a piece. As we sat there, it kind of felt like we were celebrating a new beginning on the island. I finally had that friend I'd always wanted.

After Bertram and Odin went to their living quarters for the evening, I ran as fast as I could to

Elise's room, barging in. She was sitting at a desk, looking in a lit mirror, brushing her hair.

"What are you doing here so late?" she asked, glancing over at me, surprised.

"I have a friend, Elise . . . finally!"

"Really? What do you mean?" She stopped combing her hair, stood up, and walked over to me, looking more concerned than happy.

"There's a new boy here. He's the son of someone my dad brought to the island today," I continued, so happy to share the good news.

"I didn't know we were expecting anyone. Who are you talking about?" she asked.

"The dad's name is Bertram, and the kid is Odin, and he's the best thing ever."

"Bertram?" she asked, with a scared look on her face.

"Yes, do you know him?"

"Yes, from a long time ago, actually. I haven't heard that name in a while. He's a lovely man, but

I don't know if it's good that he's arrived," she said.

"What does that mean?"

"That Gareth is out of control," she muttered, as if she couldn't help herself. I was used to her saying bad things about my dad, so I shrugged it off and kept talking.

"Anyway, I can't wait for you to meet him," I said. I knew Elise would like Odin very much. How could she not? He was serious, but he had a nice smile and seemed to like me too.

"Okay, Chelsea. Time to go to bed. I need to go speak with your father right away."

"Wait, what about? I'm not in trouble, am I?" I asked, hugging Elise and looking up at her.

"No, my dear, but you need to go to asleep. It's getting very late. I'll lead you out," she said.

I trotted out of her room to go to my bed even though I was too excited to lie down. She followed me out and walked quickly down the hall in the other direction.

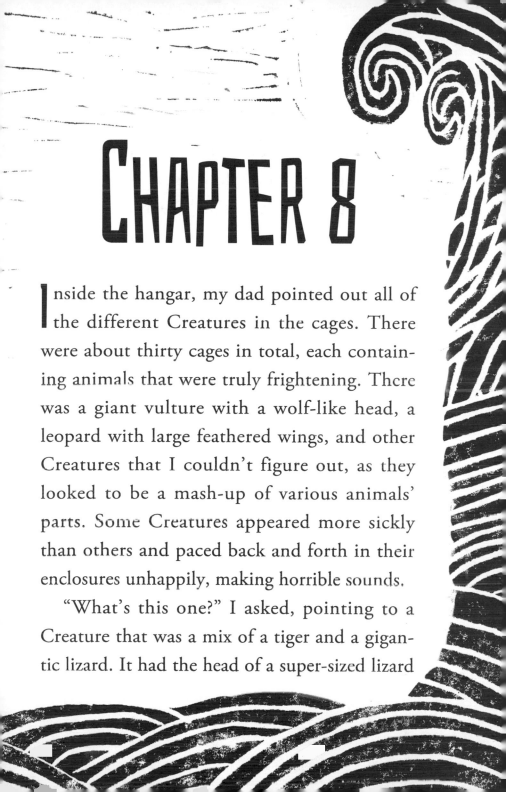

CHAPTER 8

Inside the hangar, my dad pointed out all of the different Creatures in the cages. There were about thirty cages in total, each containing animals that were truly frightening. There was a giant vulture with a wolf-like head, a leopard with large feathered wings, and other Creatures that I couldn't figure out, as they looked to be a mash-up of various animals' parts. Some Creatures appeared more sickly than others and paced back and forth in their enclosures unhappily, making horrible sounds.

"What's this one?" I asked, pointing to a Creature that was a mix of a tiger and a gigantic lizard. It had the head of a super-sized lizard but the lower body of a tiger with orange-tinged fur and black stripes. When I approached, it opened up its giant mouth and hissed at me.

"Oh that's the Komodo dragon-tiger hybrid. It's one of my favorites. This Creature possesses the speed and cunning of a tiger and the dangerous bite of a Komodo dragon. We increased the head size to be proportionate to a tiger's body—isn't that amazing? Also, did you know a Komodo's bite is venomous?"

"No, I didn't know that," feeling disturbed, but not surprised, that he was engineering these animals to be as scary as possible. "When you say we . . . who's we? Who is working on this with you?"

I guessed that he didn't create these things on his own and I wondered who was helping him.

"Oh, the scientists—"

"But who are they? Do they live among us? Do I know them?"

"Well, want to know a little secret?" he leaned

into me, eyebrows raised. I nodded. "The person who really figured out how to do this is Elise. She's the brains behind the operation."

"Wait . . . what? I thought you hated each other?" I asked, confused.

"Oh yes, we do, but she's the most talented genetic scientist I've ever met. I knew she was special when I met her so many years ago."

"So, she's still helping you with this?" I asked, feeling a little hurt that Elise kept such a huge secret from me for so long. She'd always been so honest with me.

"No, she stopped a few years ago, but the bulk of the work had been done."

"Why did she stop?"

"Well, we had different creative visions, so to speak," my dad said, smirking at me as we continued to walk from cage to cage. Some of the animals were glorious and fierce and perfectly formed, whereas others looked like they were cobbled together out of mismatched animal parts. I felt bad for all of them, stuck in the small cages. We walked toward the back, where there was a row of smaller cages. Inside, they were filled with baby Creatures and ones that looked more like adolescents. I bent down to look at a cute owl with a cat-like face, and a hippo the size of a large dog with hind legs like a wolf.

"So, why don't you get rid of Elise like everyone else that doesn't agree with you?"

It was a very forward question, but I was feeling bold given my dad's candor in the moment.

"Well, I'm hoping she'll come around again once she sees what beauty she helped create," he said as we stood in front of an animal that was composed of the body of a cheetah and the head of an alligator.

"Plus, I can't help but have a soft spot in my heart for Elise," he said.

"You have a soft spot?" I joked. He laughed and the alligator-cheetah turned and looked at him, its mouth open, exposing large, sharp teeth.

"I know, it's hard to believe, right? But that's the honest truth," he said, putting his arm around me. We stood there quietly, and I was taking everything in.

"I like this one," I said, staring at the alligator-cheetah, which was one of the most amazing animals I'd ever seen.

"So who else is helping you with this now?" I asked again. This obviously wasn't a solo operation, and I guessed there must be Suits I knew involved in this. No one had ever even hinted that these things were happening here.

"Chelsea, I have a whole team of scientists working on this program. They've been here for many, many years and are finally going to see their hard work on full display," he said.

"What does that mean?"

"Well, some of these animals will go to the game reserve area where they can be hunted—for a steep price, of course. And the very, very special ones, like this one here, I'm saving for the

Coliseum," he smiled at the thought and I knew the kids that faced these Creatures didn't stand a chance to survive.

"Dad, I have a question for you," I said, looking around at the huge space and all that he had accomplished in the hangar. He had spent years and years of time and God-knew-how-much money making it happen, but it worked.

"Yes, love?"

"How can you make new animals from scratch but you can't get me off the island? How could you possibly need more time?"

It didn't seem that complicated to me to figure out a way for me to have a life off the island, especially when compared to all the other amazing things my dad had accomplished.

"You're right, love," he said, looking sad all of a sudden. "But you are the most important person in the world to me, and I wanted to show you this. This is my life's work. It was something I *had* to share with you."

"And it's amazing," I said, knowing that's what he wanted to hear, even though I truly questioned everything. It seemed like he was toying with science and nature in ways that were irreversible.

I continued, trying to be careful so as not to anger my dad. "But, I want to experience the real world. I don't want to be here any more."

"The real world is not so great, Chelsea. I know I've said that before, but for some reason, you still want to see it. I don't get it. But, if it's that important to you, then I suppose I must support you," he said.

We were both quiet for a long time and I waited for him to elaborate.

"I've made a decision. You can join the next Praeclarus ship that goes back out to the helipad at sea, okay? There, there will be a helicopter waiting to take you to the real word, if you insist."

"When is that?" I asked. I needed specifics.

"The next visitors are arriving in a week. So,

after their stay, the boat will be leaving again. I'm realizing I can't keep you any longer," he said.

"Good," I said, appreciative that he was finally understanding me.

"Now, can you keep this a secret for a week?" he asked, pointing around the room.

"Yes, of course," I said. Who would I tell anyway? I had no friends here anymore. Odin was dead. Elise knew what was happening here. Reed and I weren't speaking. I wasn't sure which of the White Suits were on my dad's side and which were planning the revolt.

We turned and went to the door, and he shut off the lights, which seemed to amplify the howls and groans and shrieks of the animals, both well and sickly.

We walked back up the path and past Wexler, who looked at me with a leery expression.

"Don't worry friend, she's okay," my dad said, putting his arm around me and pulling me in close. "Right, my dear?"

"Yes, completely," I said, as convincingly as I could muster.

We got back to the compound area and I went back to my room and lay on my bed, staring up at the ceiling and thinking about what I'd just seen.

I never really understood Praeclarus and why my dad was involved with the group or why he built the island in the first place. But now, I wondered if my dad created it all to support these experiments on the animals and prove to everyone that he "must be a God," just like he said.

CHAPTER 9

The kids fighting each other in the Coliseum didn't happen right away. When the Coliseum was finished, initially my dad staged fights between animals, and all the members gathered to watch and place bets on the winners. It was a highlight of the island's available activities and what everyone was eager to see again on each subsequent trip.

Then, when I was eleven, there was a White Suit named Louis who tried to sneak aboard one of the Praeclarus ships as it was leaving. He was caught and beaten severely in the Coliseum for his treason, as my dad called it. When Louis was beaten, the staff was forced to sit and watch, as my dad was hell-bent on teaching everyone a lesson.

It was awful and many people were shocked, as my dad had been nothing but kind to everyone who arrived to work for him. But my dad never tolerated disobedience, and he made it understood that employment on the island was a one-way ticket.

But that first beating didn't stop Louis and he tried to escape again, this time with a co-conspirator named Eche, and they were both promptly caught again. As they were dragged off the boat back to the dock, Louis screamed over and over again that he was going to expose the island's secrets, and that he wasn't going to stop until the truth came out. At the time, everyone laughed at him and dismissed him as crazy, but now I wondered what he actually knew.

After Louis was caught the second time, my dad obviously didn't think the beating was harsh enough punishment, or maybe wanted to prove a

point to his rich friends who were concerned after the spectacle that Louis caused. They were paranoid that this guy was going to somehow escape and ruin it all.

My dad gathered all the members in the Coliseum and told them that all would be okay, and that he had an idea. He warned them it was violent, and that anyone was welcome to leave. He had another boat waiting for people who chose to avoid seeing Louis's punishment, but no one took that option.

As the Praeclarus men sat there, Louis and Eche were dragged in by Suits and made to fight each other to the death. My dad had other Suits standing by with guns, ready to shoot and kill if the men didn't cooperate.

I wasn't at any of the early fights, but that first battle quickly became a thing of legend. According to the story, Louis and Eche fought hard and long, using their hands alone, neither of them a trained fighter. It was ugly and sloppy, but the guys watching cheered just the same, fueled by drugs and alcohol that made them looser and more open to enjoy what they were watching.

Louis finally succumbed to the injuries and Eche was celebrated. He was invited to an extravagant feast with the group later that evening, even though he could barely open his mouth or eyes, which had been punched and gouged until they were bloody and swollen. After the dinner, Eche was never seen or heard from again.

Elise told me later that Dad had sat at that table, enjoying his friends' conversations immensely as they recounted the match blow-by-blow.

After that, every time a Suit would do something against my dad's increasingly strict rules, the Suit was sent to the Coliseum, until it got to the point where everyone was careful to act in line.

The Praeclarus members liked the fighting, though, and as the ranks of members slowly increased, Elise told me that my dad felt pressure to keep upping the ante with the group. He liked showing off to them.

But he needed fighters and he had to be careful about alienating the White Suits, as he didn't want his staff to turn on him. So, he built a special barracks for future fighters and kids started arriving after that.

Odin and I were curious, and we'd sneak in to go talk to them. Often, they were homeless kids, snatched off the street in the middle of the night, never to be heard from again. We'd leave their area and feel bad for them, knowing what they were going to face and feeling happy for our own freedom, even if was limited to a stretch of island that we couldn't escape.

When the kids first came, I never, ever expected Odin to become one of them.

Back then, Odin and I spent every waking moment with each other, so it was inevitable that we'd fall in love, and we both fell hard, searching the island together for the secret corners where we could be alone.

I was as happy as I'd ever been until Bertram got in trouble, changing everything completely.

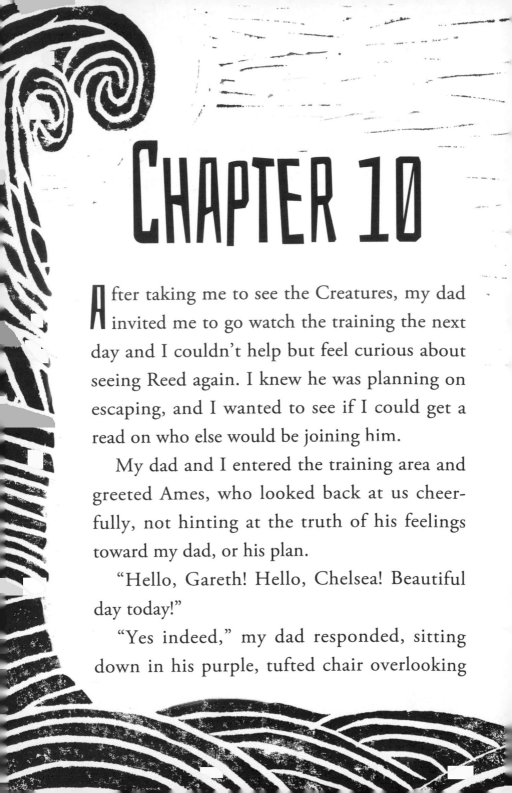

CHAPTER 10

After taking me to see the Creatures, my dad invited me to go watch the training the next day and I couldn't help but feel curious about seeing Reed again. I knew he was planning on escaping, and I wanted to see if I could get a read on who else would be joining him.

My dad and I entered the training area and greeted Ames, who looked back at us cheerfully, not hinting at the truth of his feelings toward my dad, or his plan.

"Hello, Gareth! Hello, Chelsea! Beautiful day today!"

"Yes indeed," my dad responded, sitting down in his purple, tufted chair overlooking the training area. I sat beside him and I felt all the people in the vicinity looking at me.

This was normal and something I'd grown accustomed to many years ago. People had been telling me I was beautiful for as long as I could remember. In fact, I learned to use my looks in my favor, acting coy when that was to my advantage or aggressively confident when I needed someone to bend to my wishes.

Many of the Praeclarus visitors and some of the White Suits had told me that I was the most beautiful woman they'd ever seen. Having seen so few women in real life, I didn't have a sense of whether these compliments were inflated or true, but I knew that I could command people's attention quite easily, if I wanted to.

As I sat down, I stared at Reed and smiled at him, giving a little wave in his direction, and he looked at me, confused.

To his left stood Micah, a giant but handsome goofball that seemed a waste to be contained

to this setting. He was gorgeous and smiled at me gregariously, calling out hello. In a way, he reminded me of Odin—both giant, muscular guys with a commanding presence. Odin had grown serious and angry the longer he was kept a prisoner, but Micah made me think of the Odin I once knew.

As Ames put everyone through a series of stretches and then weapons training, I watched all the kids and wondered who would face the Creature first.

I started to fixate on Delphine, watching her move quickly, her arms darting out expertly with her sword, and then her doing sideways somersaults to avoid being tackled by her practice opponent. Her skin was tanned and sweaty and her long red hair was tied back in a loose braid that swung and glinted in the sun. She told jokes as she fought and everyone else laughed with her and seemed to be on her side. She was popular among the group and when I looked over at my dad, he seemed to like what he saw as well, clapping and cheering in approval of her abilities.

The group took a water break and I noticed Delphine and Reed go off to a corner. Reed whispered something that made Delphine laugh. She rested her head on Reed's shoulder and he nuzzled his forehead against hers. Were they together? I instantly felt my anger rise up again. It was confusing and I sensed myself feeling jealous. That was the way Reed used to look at me, but now he barely glanced in my direction. The jealous impulses made me even angrier as I felt like I was betraying Odin by even having those thoughts at all.

They continued to flirt and laugh with each other until suddenly, my dad chimed in, leaning into me. "What do you think Reed is up to?"

We were both watching them and they seemed oblivious and in their own private little moment in the midst of the training.

"I have no idea," I said, trying not to sound annoyed.

Then, I had a new thought. "The crowd really loves Delphine, don't they?"

"Yes, she is one of the most popular fighters, without a doubt," my dad said, gazing at her.

"That's who you need to put in the first battle against a Creature," I said, sure this was the right answer. I had grown to be my dad's co-conspirator, helping him make these decisions before a key fight. He always valued my advice in these matters, and usually agreed. I don't know why I wanted her gone, and I regretted the suggestion as soon as I said it.

"Hmmm . . . " he said, letting out a long, heavy sigh. "I'm not so sure. I actually have other plans for her," he said.

"What do you mean?" I asked. I didn't like how that sounded. Usually when my dad had plans, not any good came from them.

"Ames! Ames!" my dad yelled, and Ames came jogging over, looking eager to help him.

"Yes, Gareth?"

"Bring me Delphine," he instructed, and Ames raised his eyebrows. "Isn't she a little young?" he asked in a joking way, glancing back to where Delphine and Reed were standing.

"According to island law, that is old enough," he said, and "island law" always won out. I grew up with my dad's particular rules, and had seen him with young women before.

Ames turned around and walked over to Delphine, saying something I couldn't hear from this distance. She looked back and shook her head and I heard her cry, "No. No way. No."

My dad kind of laughed and Reed tried to step in, but Ames shot him a look and shoved him away hard.

Ames dragged Delphine to our side of the training area, up the stairs, and into the box where we sat.

She reluctantly sat down and my dad said to her, "Don't worry. I don't bite, my dear. Lucky you, I saved you from the next battle, actually."

Delphine just glared back at him and refused to speak.

"Chelsea here wanted to send you to fight first, but I saved you," my dad continued, looking over at me and smiling. I protested, annoyed that he called me out. Delphine just rolled her eyes.

"That's interesting. Are you jealous?" she asked, glaring at me.

"Now, now, let's everyone be civil. We're all going to have to get along. Delphine, you're now my guest of honor and I'll take care of you, don't you worry."

"Let me out of here," she spat at him.

"You know I can't do that, but I will make you feel like a princess," my dad said. Delphine tried to move her body away from his, but my dad's hand was firmly squeezing her thigh. I looked up at the four Suits that surrounded us, and they were all smirking at each other.

"I don't want that," she said.

"Shh . . . darling. Now, we'll escort you to your room to get cleaned and dressed up, and I'll meet you for a special dinner, just you and I, so we can get to know each other better," he said.

I looked down and saw Reed watching everything, anger etched on his face. He kind of seemed pitiful, not able to take any action to help his friend or girlfriend or whatever Delphine was to him.

I did feel bad for Delphine in a way because when it came to women, my dad was a creep. He had temporary fixations, where he'd fall in love with someone—a Suit or a fighter or one of the designated female companions—madly and intensely for a very short period of time, and then disregard them completely, often reassigning them to the island's worst job duties.

But when someone new captured his attention, he insisted they spend nearly every waking minute with him, and would swear up and down that this new one was *the one*—his island life partner forever more.

"Now, I think I've gotten everything I need out of this training session," my dad said, taking Delphine by the hand and leading her down the stairs to exit. She looked back toward Reed, terrified.

"But Dad, you didn't figure out who is going to be in the next battle," I said.

He just looked at me and smirked. "Oh, don't worry, I've made a decision. I think the next fight will be especially dramatic for everyone," he said, and laughed to himself.

Maybe he was going to take my advice after all and put Delphine in the ring, and this was just a ruse or a game of some sort. I knew it wasn't normal to wish death on anyone, and yet, I wanted her gone, and that impulse scared me.

Did my genetic connection to my father make me someone who had these types of thoughts?

I knew I had to fight those impulses.

I looked down and watched Reed as he was beckoned over by Ames, who put his arm on his shoulder and was saying something to him that I couldn't hear.

Ames looked very serious and I'm sure he was telling Reed that he just needed to hang on for a little longer, which is what everyone said on the island. Up to this point, that hadn't helped anyone at all. Elise hung on and she was still here, I hung on and Odin was dead, Reed hung on and Delphine had been taken away.

Reed turned his head up toward me and looked me straight in the eye. For once, I felt shy and quickly got up, rushing out, unsure what to do next.

CHAPTER 11

Praeclarus members always arrived on Saturdays. On those mornings, the boats pulled up to the dock, one after another. They were all staffed and chartered by Suits, for security measures.

On arrival days, my dad always made me go sit by the pool to hold court and chat with the members, most of whom I'd known since I was a very little girl. I was aware that they were very famous and powerful in the real world, and the majority spoke at least broken English, so I'd hobble through conversations with them, asking them about what they'd been up to since their last visit. I knew better than to ask about wives or kids—even though I'd been tempted to so many times. Those types of questions were just unsavory reminders of the lives they left behind to enjoy everything the island had to offer.

On this day, the weather was perfect, with pretty blue skies and I wore my short, pink sundress that Odin loved. I sat on a lounge chair at the end of the pool and fantasized that one way or another, I'd be off this island soon enough.

If I joined the revolt and managed to escape, I'd enter the real world without my dad's support, without money, and without any knowledge about how to survive. Hopefully Elise and Ames could guide me, but that was no guarantee.

And what about Reed? Could he help me? We were the same age and I remember he talked about Oregon, which sounded like a nice place. I wondered if I could go home with him, if we ever got out of here. His life back at home seemed good, even if he had issues with his own father. I knew in my heart that Elise was right that my anger

toward him was misplaced. I started to feel the familiar tug of doubt toward my father and his intentions.

Even though I was supposed to be by the pool this morning to greet everyone, I needed to go find Reed and talk to him. Would he help me if I joined the revolt and tried to escape with them? Would he trust me?

I stood up and went to the training area, where they'd be at this time of day. I went down the hallways and got to the arena, where everyone stopped to say hello. Ames looked surprised to see me when I walked in.

"Aren't you supposed to be at the pool today?"

"Yes, but I don't care about that right now."

I scanned the group of kids, who were busy grappling with each other.

"Where's Reed?" I asked.

Ames broke away from the group and came over to stand right next to me so we could talk quietly.

"Why are you asking for Reed?" he questioned, raising his eyebrows. "I thought you hated him?"

"I did, but I need to talk to him," I said. "Don't worry, I'm not out to get him or you."

"Well, it's too late. He's been taken away to prep for this afternoon's battle. Gareth's orders. And Gareth made me stay behind today . . . I think he might be on to us," he said. "Did you tell him about our plans?"

"No. I didn't say a thing."

My heart sank immediately hearing that Reed had been chosen for the round. That meant he was the one my dad chose to face a Creature. And I didn't think it was possible for any human to survive that, no matter how much they'd trained. He'd be ripped apart.

"What's wrong?" Ames asked.

"Reed's in trouble today," I said. "Do you know where he was taken?"

"No idea. Check the prep rooms. What are you talking about?" he asked.

"I don't have time. I need to talk to Reed," I said as I turned and ran out, rushing to search all the possible rooms where they might be holding Reed before the fight.

I sprinted past White Suits and Praeclarus members who greeted me, and I ignored their puzzled stares. I looked in each prep room and holding area, unable to locate Reed anywhere.

I finally went to find my dad, who was now sitting by the pool with Delphine by his side, and five Praeclarus members gathered around. The men were all laughing hard at some story my dad was telling.

As I approached, Delphine pulled her body away from my dad as he wrapped his arm around her shoulder. She looked pretty, but bored—or miserable—I couldn't tell. She had on makeup, her hair was brushed and clean, and she was wearing a nice outfit. I could see the men gazing at her like she was something to be taken, and when I walked up they all turned and smiled at me.

"Chelsea! We've been waiting for you!" my dad said, grinning widely but looking angry all the same. I knew that fake smile all too well.

"Where have you been?"

"I was feeling sick," I said, which was partially true.

"Well, go get dressed. Today's battle starts in an hour, and this is one I don't want you to miss," he said, winking at me, and pulling Delphine even closer in, giving her a big kiss on the cheek.

I wanted to blurt out to Delphine what was about to happen, but knew that I'd probably be barred from attending the fight if I acted out. And I didn't want to let on to my dad that my allegiance was shifting. I needed him to think I was in on his plan to get me out of here. Who knows what he'd do if I turned on him, too.

I went to my room, got dressed, and prayed that Reed would find a way out of the Coliseum alive today.

CHAPTER 12

After putting on my white dress, I headed to the Coliseum, passing excited White Suits and Praeclarus members who were headed in the same direction. There were rumors that something special was happening at today's fight, so I heard excited chatter and speculation among groups that I passed. Of course, I knew that they had absolutely no idea of the truth. How could one even imagine it?

I wondered if it was wise of my dad to bring the Creatures to light. This type of development could make people a lot of money, I guessed. Some might think it a waste to restrict the animals to this little island where they'd never see the real world—or their true earning potential.

My dad was obsessed with continuously raising the stakes with his friends, and proving he was better and more powerful than them; but I knew this couldn't last forever, and today might be the tipping point where his secrets wouldn't remain on the island any longer. I imagined that he was opening a Pandora's box by letting his monsters out to play.

My dad thought he had it all together, though. He had gone through many precautions to protect the island—I'd heard rumors of GPS encryption and surveillance, patrol boats, and more, but I knew he couldn't protect against one of the Praeclarus members turning on him. Even he described the island being ruled by an honor system with the highest of stakes.

I entered the Coliseum and even though I'd seen the view thousands of times, it still took my breath away. It was so beautiful, crafted out of

white marble. My dad spent millions of dollars getting it shipped from Italy.

Many people were already in their seats and turned to look at me as I entered. I smiled, not wanting to show my true anxiety about what we were about to witness. I walked up the stairs to where my dad sat with Delphine by his side. She was wearing a bright, silk emerald gown that complemented her complexion.

I sat down in my usual spot next to my dad, and he looked over and smiled at me.

"You ready for this?" he asked. I nodded and forced my most convincing smile.

After all the Praeclarus members, their "companions," and White Suits were seated, my dad began to speak, his tanned face projecting on the large screen over the far Coliseum wall.

"Welcome, ladies and gentlemen, to a very special day, one unlike any previous battle I've hosted before," he said, and then paused for dramatic effect as the crowd's cheers rose up around us.

"I've spent my whole life working on a project that I'm ready to debut for you, my dearest friends," he continued. "With the help of a small team, we've pushed the limits of human endeavor and have accomplished something thought to be limited to the world of fantasies. And what you'll see today is the future on the island. Something only you—this small, select group—is privy to witness and enjoy."

This of course, made all the fat and sweaty men, half-dressed women, and Suits cheer even louder as they all loved nothing more than the exclusivity of the experiences my dad created here.

"Well, I think you'll be pleased to see who I've chosen to debut in this special experience. I had to pick a fighter that was worthy of the challenge I'm presenting to you today. And who else, but the boy who took out our greatest fighter, Odin?"

I cringed and felt sick to my stomach hearing the reference to Odin, and being reminded so publicly what happened to him. My dad didn't seem to care enough to think it might bother me, and the screen then cut to my face. The crowd cheered, and I faked a smile and waved. Give them what they want, of course.

The camera then panned to Delphine, with the goal of showcasing her beauty, I'm sure, but she just looked upset and was glaring over at my dad, causing the camera to cut back to him quickly.

"Reed? Not Reed again!" Delphine protested, which was picked up by my dad's mic.

"Without further adieu, let's bring him out. The man of the hour," my dad said. "Maybe he'll be the first one to earn the ten-win pass out of here. Odin was so, so close, but Reed, I think he's got a shot. Except today's going to be a tough one, right, Chelsea?"

"Yes, should be very challenging indeed," I said, playing the part.

The gate lifted and Reed came out, walking without a struggle between two Suits that looked very serious. He knew that it was fruitless to try to escape here, I was sure, and he stood with his shoulders back and head lifted, having no idea what he was about to face. He was becoming a better and more assured fighter. He carried his long sharp dagger with a red ruby-lined handle that gleamed in the sun.

Delphine screamed down, "Reed! Reed! We'll get out of here together. You can do this!"

This just made my dad smile even wider. Reed glanced up at her and nodded.

The sun shone down on him. He was shirtless, his body more chiseled with each appearance in the ring. He was undeniably handsome. Smaller than Odin, he still carried himself with a similar assuredness that I found appealing, despite myself.

CHAPTER 13

T he gate rose again and a squadron of Suits pushed a large, black metal cage on wheels into the ring. The camera zoomed in and I finally made out what was inside.

It was the Komodo dragon and tiger hybrid, one of the prized Creatures my dad had shown me in the hangar. The men and women in the crowd started talking excitedly to each other, their voices a loud buzz all around me. They were probably unsure of what they were seeing, and if their eyes were playing tricks on them.

Reed backed up a few steps as the cage was rolled in, and looked scared.

"What is that?" Delphine demanded to my dad.

"The future, my dear, and you're in the best seat in the house to witness it." He stood up to the crowd. "So, is your curiosity piqued?" he asked, making everyone go wild. "I don't want to leave you waiting a moment longer. Why don't we let the games begin," he ordered, causing the Suits on the Coliseum floor to scurry away behind the closing gates.

My dad held a small device in his hand and pressed a button, causing the cage's door to automatically open. The Creature inside took a step forward slowly at first, out of the cage and into plain sight, where everyone could view it in its full glory.

The animal had a large tiger body with sharp claws and a tiger's tufted fur neck, but its head was that of a giant lizard, with beady black eyes. There was a collar around its neck that appeared to be lit up red, and I wondered what it was for.

The animal stood about thirty yards from Reed and didn't look particularly aggressive at the moment. It sniffed the air and looked up at the sunlight—something I gathered it had never seen before.

The crowd screamed and all stared, transfixed, turning their heads to the screen and the floor.

"What you see there is what happens when you combine and tweak the genetic codes of a Komodo dragon and a Bengal tiger." My dad narrated as everyone clapped wildly, witnessing something that was truly, by definition, extraordinary.

"It's fast and clever like a tiger, with the vicious bite of a Komodo dragon. Pretty incredible, right?" he asked. Everyone went crazy cheering in agreement.

Reed stood in a fighter's pose, trying to brace himself for what was to happen next. He bent his legs and raised the dagger, which looked wimpy compared to the Creature's mouth of sharp teeth, plainly visible every time the Creature hissed.

"Well, are we ready to see what this beauty can do?" my dad asked and everyone yelled out in support. Dad raised the device in his hand and pressed a button, which emitted a loud zapping sound from the animal's collar, causing it to yelp loudly with a strange, guttural sound.

It took a step forward in Reed's direction and Delphine cried out.

"Oh God no!"

I felt helpless, knowing there wasn't anything I could do to prevent what was about to happen.

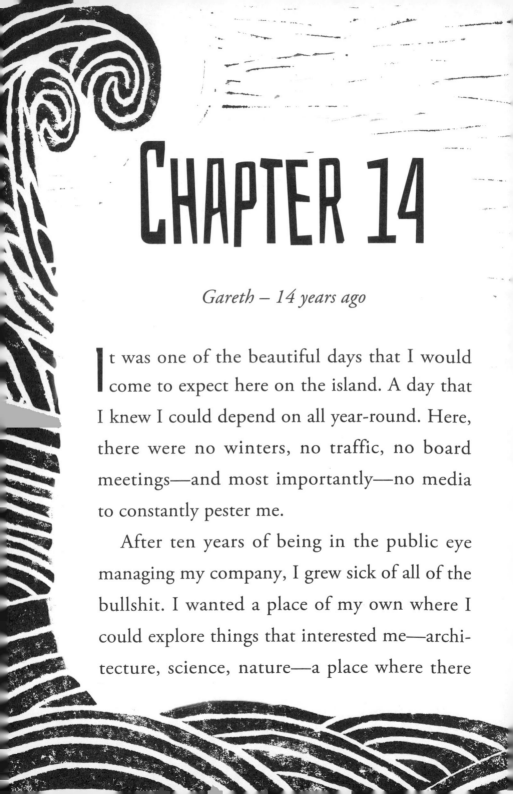

CHAPTER 14

Gareth — 14 years ago

It was one of the beautiful days that I would come to expect here on the island. A day that I knew I could depend on all year-round. Here, there were no winters, no traffic, no board meetings—and most importantly—no media to constantly pester me.

After ten years of being in the public eye managing my company, I grew sick of all of the bullshit. I wanted a place of my own where I could explore things that interested me—architecture, science, nature—a place where there were no rules except the ones I created based on principles that I cared about.

I'd been invited to join Praeclarus five years ago. When I was approached about it, I was surprised as it was something I didn't know existed before the invite was extended. I paid investigators five hundred thousand dollars to find out as much as they could about the group, but their search yielded absolutely nothing. It was like it didn't exist at all.

This intrigued me even more, and I accepted the invitation, knowing that if it was that mysterious, I wanted to be a part of this very exclusive secret society.

It was an honor, of course, to be chosen as a member among some of the richest, most powerful people in the world.

Back in those early days, Praeclarus met up for retreats a few times a year. We'd all let loose a bit without fear of being caught and exposed by the media. I loved it, but I wanted to go off the grid

completely and live in a place where the ideals of practices of Praeclarus, as I envisioned them, could be realized year-round.

I searched a long time for a piece of land that I could develop from scratch and protect from detection using the technologies my company had created. When I finally found the uninhabited island, I knew it was what I had been searching for. It was in a remote area of the Indian Ocean, far away from shipping channels.

It was exceedingly difficult to get to, unless, of course, you were invited.

I paid a very select group of people to build up the island for me with its first buildings, and when it was ready, Elise and I took a vacation by private plane, which crashed, according to media reports.

It was funny, seeing your own death all over the media while sitting by a pool drinking a scotch, and knowing you pulled off your plan successfully. It was almost too easy. Elise and I were in love and we had a whole future filled with remarkable ideas about what we wanted to accomplish together on the island. I was dazzled by her mind and her scientific capabilities.

I recruited top scientists to come join us, also faking their deaths and disappearances, and I paid each handsomely to come live with us here, in our own private Utopia. I chose carefully, based on people who could be lured away from their comfortable lives for good.

For enough money and with utmost discretion, anyone who I wanted to be bought could be.

So as Elise and I sat on the beach some time after we'd settled on the island, I was frustrated to be fighting yet again.

"I thought it was clear what we were trying to accomplish here?" I asked her, and she shook her head angrily.

"No, Gareth, I didn't sign up for this, and you know it," she spat at me, tossing her dark hair over her shoulder. Even when she was mad, she was the most beautiful and impressive woman I'd ever known, and I reached over to kiss her tanned shoulder. She pulled away.

We watched Chelsea kneeling down, building a sand castle and looking over at us. She was just a toddler, but she seemed to be listening in to our conversation, watching us with a serious expression.

"Sweetie, can you go collect some shells? There's a bunch over there," Elise said, pointing down the beach, and Chelsea ran with her bucket to go grab them.

"I think you're doing this to impress your Praeclarus buddies," Elise said. "Weren't we going to work on projects to better the world? Here, with no distractions? I thought that was the long-term plan. That's what you promised me."

"We are, love. The specimens we've developed are going to show people that there are no limits to human creativity and scientific advances, and you're at the forefront of all of that."

"But, how will we ever share it? The things we

are doing here are illegal and possibly immoral, and we're fugitives here, and can't escape. You know it. I want out of here, Gareth," she said.

I was disgusted by what she was saying. We'd committed to this journey together and had worked tirelessly together on the many imperfect iterations of our Creatures, and suddenly she was getting cold feet.

"What? You know that's not possible. Where would you go? You're nothing out there. What would you do? You're penniless without me. And as far as the world knows, you're long dead," I said.

I knew the words were cruel, but she wasn't leaving, so I had to be harsh. I knew she'd try to take Chelsea with her. And, I still needed Elise. She'd made so many amazing developments already with our project, but we still had a lot of work to do. My vision wasn't complete.

"What can I do to make you happy?" I asked, trying to reason with her. Chelsea was down the beach, singing to herself and putting shells in her bucket, and then pouring them out, over and over again.

"Let us go. Create a new life for us and let me leave here," she pleaded.

"I can't do that—not yet. But one day, after I've ensured my plans have come to fruition and I don't need you anymore, then, yes, I'll help you," I said reluctantly.

We sat in silence, watching the water lap onto the shore. We were in a protected bay, and it was one of the prettiest spots on the island. We used to spend time here every day when we first arrived, but it happened less and less as time went on, and we began spending more time apart than together. We'd had versions of this conversation so many times and I was growing tired of it.

"Listen. Once I'm certain I have no more use for your scientific insights, then you can go. I promise. I need you until then. This is my lifelong dream. Please help to make it come true," I asked. Elise looked frustrated, but nodded.

"I have nothing more to offer you, Gareth."

"Yes. I know you don't love me any longer." I said.

It was true, and the feeling was mutual. But I needed her and I wasn't going to let her go. Years before, I got it into my mind to try to create scientific mutations like what I'd read about in mythology books when I was a boy. It was a fantasy to see that come to life—and why not?—I had the funds and the resources to make it a reality. It would just take time, determination, and talented scientists, all of which I had at my disposal here on the island. And we'd made so much progress already.

"What are you doing with your fantasies about the Coliseum—really?" she asked suddenly. "Why consider building that if you're not staging fights?"

She knew me better than anyone else, I think,

and I couldn't help but smirk at her. Of course it wasn't going to be just an empty monument, not to be used. I was going to give Praeclarus members even more than they knew they wanted to see.

I had very big ideas.

I was going to start shipping exotic creatures to the island—not just for use by Elise in her experiments, but also to fight each other in the ring. When the Coliseum was ready, I'd debut the animal fights. I toyed with the idea of animals even fighting humans, something I'd never seen before.

That would be cool, wouldn't it? And here, it would be okay, because I made the rules.

I wasn't sure who the fighters would be though—they'd have to be criminals, I thought, to get my Praeclarus members on board watching humans fight—or staff that broke the rules.

The members would need to be in on the plan to enjoy it, so they'd come back for more, and so they'd keep my secrets.

Any new Praeclarus members were chosen carefully and vetted thoroughly to ensure their moral compass wasn't guided necessarily by standards set by current society. We all shared the desire for discretion above all else, so I wasn't too worried, but knew I'd have to approach the next stages of my plan and the fights with caution.

"Elise, you know how much I enjoy classical architecture," I said, and although this was true, we both understood my dreams were bigger than just erecting buildings, even if I wouldn't say it outright.

"This is no place for a young girl to grow up, Gareth," she said in response, changing subjects.

I didn't agree. This was a magical place for a kid.

"What are you talking about? Look around. This is paradise, actually. Chelsea can safely explore mountains and forests and beaches and create her own adventures in the wild—a new one every day. This is a better childhood than being raised in front of TVs and being disconnected by cell phones and social networks and shit like that," I said while she just shook her head.

When Elise got pregnant, it was a surprise and we discussed all of these ideas. I thought the island was a beautiful place for a child. I'd give Chelsea everything she ever wanted and she'd want for nothing.

"But what about friends? She'll have none here," Elise said. "A girl needs companions her own age."

"We'll be her friends, or I'll bring more kids here."

"What are you talking about? Whose kids? You can't just steal kids away, you know."

"You're right. I'll bring new staffers in with kids."

"You cannot do that. That would be disastrous," Elise warned. "It is not okay to bring other children into these circumstances in which they'll never be able to leave. Everyone who comes to the island should come by choice."

Elise was the overly cautious one, which annoyed me sometimes. Everyone else on the island was there on their own accord—I recruited staff that wanted to be there and I was always perfectly clear that if they chose to come here, there was no turning back. A ticket to this place was a gift when compared to where many of the staff had come from.

"So, you're going to let me go?" Elise finally asked, exasperated. "I'm not going to forget this conversation, you know."

"Yes, as soon as you fulfill your obligation. You realize I can't let you go until then. And, if you try to push the issue any more, I'm going to have to kill you," I said quietly so Chelsea couldn't overhear us. "I'll tie weights to your ankles and send you on a one-way boat ride if I have to."

I needed to strike fear in her so she'd stay in line.

She sighed heavily and stared off at the water.

"Okay, Gareth. You have a deal."

I knew this bit of hope would make her more amenable to helping me in the future, if it came to that.

"Chelsea, come here, love," Elise called out. Our little girl picked up the heavy bucket and dragged it toward us, smiling wildly. She was a gorgeous creature and full of a joy I wanted to feel too.

"Mama! Dada! Look!" she said, emptying out the bucket and showing us a starfish with seven legs, different from the rest.

It seemed like a sign, somehow, and I laughed. "Why, isn't that something?" I said, holding up the creature and showing Elise, who rolled her eyes and got up, shaking off sand from her perfect behind.

CHAPTER 15

Chelsea – Age 12

"I'm bored. What are we going to do today?" I whined to Odin. We were floating in inner tubes in the pool, the light waves rippling across the water and pushing us into each other. Each time our legs grazed, a strange jolt rushed through my body and I felt myself blush. I hoped he didn't notice and I looked over shyly, embarrassed that my friend was making me nervous.

"I don't know," Odin said, gazing at me. "This is pretty nice."

"I want to get in some trouble—don't you?"

I asked, peeking at him with a smirk. "Can't you surprise me with an adventure? Something we've never done before?"

I was challenging him, knowing he liked to make me happy and he'd figure something out. We were quiet for a minute.

"Hmm . . . well, I do have an idea of something new, but you're going to have to be brave," he said, and gave me that mischievous look that I liked. Our dads were upstairs in their office working on some project that we didn't understand. Every time we tried to spy on them, they caught on, shut their computers, and told us to go away because they were working.

Odin was my only friend and I depended on him to create fun and excitement for me, so I was happy that he seemed up for mischief.

Odin and I had spent every day together since he arrived, and we had explored the entire island. He helped me map out the land perfectly—that took us many months. Being the artist, I drew everything carefully, taking time to count out the distance between each landmark with my feet, which I used as a unit of measurement on the map's key.

I drew out every path, each bench, even the large boulders and small buildings—in pencil first, then black ink. We had to do it many times over, as the first versions were out of proportion, and Odin always encouraged me and helped me figure out how to improve it until finally, on our sixth try, we pinned the map to the wall in my bedroom to check it out. It was quite large, and we took a step back and looked at it together.

"It's perfect," Odin assured me as he put his arm around me, and I felt that rush for the first time. I was starting to have a major crush on him. At least, that's what I thought it was although it was my first time I'd ever liked someone, so I couldn't be sure. When I told Elise about it, she smiled and thought it was wonderful news, giving me a hug.

For two years, I felt increasingly sure that I loved him, but I had no idea how to say it. In my gut, I knew that this was what love felt like, and it was amazing and painful at the same time.

So that day, of course I wanted nothing more than to get in trouble with him. He was the most fun person to do anything with, especially when we were up to no good. I liked that rush of adrenaline and laughing with him when we were somewhere doing something our dads wouldn't approve of.

"With my plan," Odin said, smiling at me, "we can't do anything until after everyone else is asleep, but I promise it will be worth it. Go get some rest now and then meet me at the bottom of the mountain path at midnight," he said as he helped me out of the pool and handed me a towel, wrapping it around me and patting my back.

"The mountain path?" I asked, raising my eyebrows at him and smiling. That sounded promising.

I went up to my room and tried to rest, but I was too excited. At dinner, I sat quietly and when my dad asked me questions, I was distracted. I pretended to go to bed and when it got close to midnight, I put on my favorite outfit of my white sundress and blue cardigan, excited to see what Odin had up his sleeve.

When it was time, I snuck out to the pathway and in the moon's light, I saw Odin standing in a fitted t-shirt; I tried to look cool.

"Are you nervous?" he asked.

"No. Why would I be?" I shot back. He laughed.

"So, where are we going?"

"Follow me," he said, grabbing my hand and leading me on the path that led to the mountain. He gave me a flashlight and we walked arm in arm, giggling with each other as we stumbled over rocks and roots that popped up out of the pathway. When the path forked and we went right, I finally knew where we were heading.

"Why are you taking me to the reserve?" I asked. It was a place we had been countless times before and I thought we were doing something new and fun.

"Just wait. I want to show you something."

We approached the large fence in the area where the tiger was held. As we pointed the flashlight toward him, we saw that he was pacing back and forth on the far end of the enclosure. When he spotted us, he stopped in his tracks and stared at us without moving.

"And . . . what are we doing here?"

I still wasn't convinced this was anything fun.

"Check this out," Odin said and walked up to the metal gate with the keypad on it. He opened it up and started to press a series of numbers into it.

"Hey, what are you doing?" I asked, confused. Neither of us knew the codes to enter the enclosure; Bertram and my dad closely guarded those.

But, to my surprise, the door buzzed and Odin

pulled it open. He walked into the enclosure and turned back to me, expectantly.

"How did—" I started.

"Don't worry about that. I just found some top secret intel, and knew you'd think this was cool. You coming?" he asked, reaching out his hand.

"Are you crazy?" I hissed, and didn't know what to do. The tiger was about fifty yards away. It was insane to choose to be in the same area as it, but I also didn't want to look like a chicken. With Odin, I always tried to seem as cool and confident as possible, but this really sounded like a stupid idea.

"Don't worry, I brought this," he said as he lifted up his shirt and revealed he had tucked a gun into his belt.

"Whoa! Where'd you get that?" I asked. The only place with guns on the island was the hunting equipment room, which was also guarded by a code.

"Let's just say, after years of trying, I finally broke the code," he smiled. "Now get in here."

Not wanting to look stupid, I walked in.

The tiger seemed to be minding its own business on the other side, but when I lifted the flashlight in his direction, I saw he was still staring at us, dead still. The moonlight cast a pale blue glow over everything.

I stood next to Odin and looked around. There was no one else up here but him and me, and it was exciting to be so close to the tiger without a giant fence separating us. My heart was pounding furiously in my chest and I felt my whole body shaking in fear.

"If I run to the other end and touch the fence, then come back, what will you give me?"

"I don't know. What do you want?" I asked, feeling stupid not knowing what he was getting at.

"A kiss," he said.

I looked up at him, surprised, and wondered if he was joking, but I could tell he was serious. He didn't need to take me here to ask me that, but it seemed like he wanted to prove something to me.

"Uhh—okay—yes—" I stammered, feeling my face turn bright red as he laughed. "But what about the cameras?" I pointed up to the security cameras that were aimed at the center of the enclosure. They'd surely pick up Odin running across the field, and then we'd both be grounded forever and not allowed to see each other probably for weeks, if not longer.

"Ha ha ha, you're funny, Chelsea. No one looks at that footage. Well, no one reviews it unless something bad happens. Now, take this," he ordered and handed the gun to me, which I held in my right hand, with the flashlight in the left. "Only use it if necessary, and I hope you are a good shot," he joked, before all of a sudden taking off in a slow run, then jogging faster and faster until he was sprinting toward the wall where the tiger was standing, watching him approach.

Odin got to the far fence and hit it with his

hand, and it made a loud, clanging noise. "I did it!" he yelled out and quickly looked at the tiger, which stood unmoving, his ears flat.

As Odin turned to run back toward me, he laughed, and I laughed too. It was incredible watching him be so brave and I couldn't believe he actually wanted a kiss—from me. When he was about twenty yards away, I pointed the flashlight in his direction and suddenly I saw the tiger lunge and start running toward us in long, powerful strides. Its snarl pierced the quiet air, and I felt frozen and terrified.

I screamed "Odin! Watch out!"

But it was too late; the tiger jumped forward and with both paws, knocked Odin forcefully to the ground, causing him to scream out in pain.

The animal then pounced on top of Odin, dug his claws into Odin's shoulders, and put his mouth on his back. Odin tried to scramble away but he couldn't move.

I didn't believe what I was seeing and I quickly raised the gun.

"Chelsea. Help me!" Odin screamed and without thinking for another second, I pulled the trigger once. The gunshot rang through the air and caused me to fall backwards. The tiger howled in pain, and I saw the bullet had hit him squarely in its back. I aimed and pulled the trigger again, this time striking the tiger's leg, and then once more, shooting it in the back of the head.

The animal yelped out a God-awful noise I'd never heard before and released Odin from his grip. It looked at me in surprise, stumbled to the left, and collapsed on the ground, barely moving.

Odin lay on the ground, moaning in pain. I dropped the gun and ran up to him, horrified to see what I might find. He was alive, but his arms were bloodied and when he turned to his side, I saw that he was badly injured. I needed to get him help right away.

I knew there was only one person I could take

him to. If my dad or Bertram found out, we'd probably never get to be together again.

It was my dad's only rule about our friend-ship—we didn't get into trouble together. This was as bad as it could be. I looked over at the tiger and knew it was dead.

"Come on," I said, lifting Odin up. He cried out in pain. "I need to take you to Elise right away and we gotta get out of here quickly in case some-one heard the shots," I said. He couldn't protest as he knew I was right.

We hobbled back up the path quickly, Odin moaning in pain with nearly every step.

The path was dark and barely lit, and thank-fully, we didn't encounter anyone. We got to Elise's door and I knocked, but there was no response. I knocked again.

Finally, she opened up the door. She looked half-asleep, but quickly went wide-eyed when she saw us.

"Oh my God. What happened?"

"Just let us in. You need to help him," I cried, and we pushed in. She slammed the door behind us and made Odin take off his shirt and lay down on a towel on her bed.

The wounds were deep, but she retrieved her medical kit and spent hours stitching him back up while he moaned in pain. I explained everything and she looked at both of us with disgust.

"You're very lucky both of you weren't killed," she said, stating the obvious to me as she shook her head in disbelief.

"I know."

Odin was starting to regain color in his face, and I sat beside him, holding his hand.

After she was done stitching him up, Elise looked very concerned.

"I need to go to Bertram about this," she said.

"No, please," Odin said, as he knew his dad would be very angry, or worse, extremely disappointed in him.

"I must. There's the security footage. He's

going to have to erase it," she explained. I knew she was right. Bertram would protect Odin, which he always did before whenever we did silly, stupid things.

My dad was going to be absolutely livid about us doing something so reckless, and that his most prized tiger was killed by our dumb actions. My dad's temper was terrible and I didn't want to see what he'd do to Odin. Maybe he'd be beaten, just like others that disobeyed the island rules. I couldn't bear the thought.

When Elise left, Odin looked at me and smiled ever so slightly. "I'm so sorry to drag you into this mess," he said.

"It's okay. It was kind of exciting for a moment, wasn't it?" I joked and he sort of laughed, but it must've been painful as he stopped abruptly and groaned.

"But, at least I get a kiss out of this," he said, looking at me as my heart beat like crazy in my chest.

"Yes, that's true," I said and felt my own surge of bravery as I leaned in and kissed him long and hard. It felt like everything in my world became better in that moment.

I loved him; I knew this without a doubt. And in that moment, I was sure he loved me too.

Chapter 16

When Elise got back from talking to Bertram about the dead tiger, she insisted we take Odin back to his room to let him recover. She instructed him to pretend he had the flu, and to not come out of his room until she or Bertram told him it was safe and when everything had blown over.

I was forbidden to go visit him too, and we used the excuse that he was too sick to have visitors except Elise, who'd make sure he was okay and that his wounds were healing without infection.

In the morning, a Suit came to my room and knocked on the door. I opened it and pretended to look surprised.

"Hi there," I said. "What's up?"

"Your dad wants to see you right away," he said.

"About what?" I asked, looking as clueless as I could muster, even though my heart pounded in my chest.

"I have no idea, but he said it was urgent and not to let you stop anywhere on the way to his quarters," he said, shrugging.

"Oh, okay."

I tried to seem clueless and followed him. We walked quickly and he tried to start a conversation with me about his breakfast, but I was too nervous to really respond.

We got to my dad's quarters and the Suit led me into the room, where my dad was sitting at his desk, with Bertram perched anxiously on a chair across from him. Bertram turned to look at me as I walked in and I smiled at him as if nothing had happened at all. He smiled back but I could plainly read the disappointment in his eyes.

"Chelsea, sit down," my dad commanded. I came and sat in the chair next to Bertram.

"Yes, Dad. What's up?" I asked, looking at him with the cutest, most innocent gaze I could muster. It was one I'd practiced many times and usually worked to help me get my way.

"Someone killed my tiger last night and I wanted to see if you know anything about this," he asked, looking at me sternly.

"What are you talking about? The tiger is dead?"

I sounded shocked and upset.

"Yes, someone shot it, and so now we're interviewing everyone on the island to try to get to the bottom of it. Where were you last night?"

"In my room, of course!"

"So you didn't see or hear anything unusual last night? A few Suits thought they heard gun shots, but you didn't?" he stared at me, as if daring me to break eye contact. I didn't look away.

"No, nothing at all," I responded, shifting my weight in my seat and feeling Bertram staring at me.

"Nothing at all? Are you telling me the truth?"

"Yes, why would I lie? I'd never hurt the tiger, and I have no idea who would," I said, and it sounded a little defensive.

"Hmmm . . . that is strange indeed," my dad continued. "It's funny, because Bertram and I reviewed the security footage and it's all scrambled, and we can't make out anything at all, anywhere on the island, actually. From eight p.m. to six a.m. That is bizarre, isn't it?"

"Yes, that seems like a weird coincidence," I agreed. Bertram agreed as well.

"And now, I learn that Odin has fallen ill and no one can be around him because he's very contagious. But, I know the two of you were together yesterday, as I saw you swimming in the pool," my dad said slowly, leaning in and searching my face. "So, it makes me wonder . . ."

He said these words very slowly and I felt ill, having a good idea where this conversation was heading.

"... if this is all just a big cover up?" There was a long silence and my dad looked at me, and then at Bertram.

"Okay, okay," Bertram finally said. "I'll tell you the truth." He seemed scared. What was he going to say?

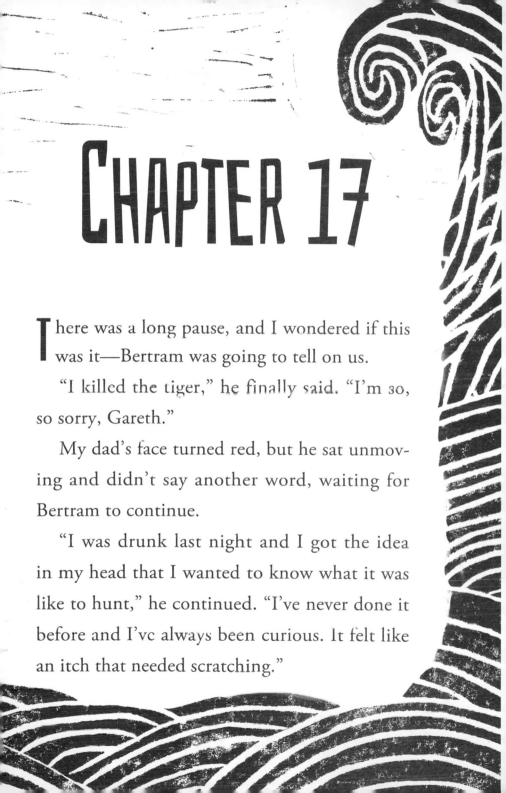

CHAPTER 17

There was a long pause, and I wondered if this was it—Bertram was going to tell on us.

"I killed the tiger," he finally said. "I'm so, so sorry, Gareth."

My dad's face turned red, but he sat unmoving and didn't say another word, waiting for Bertram to continue.

"I was drunk last night and I got the idea in my head that I wanted to know what it was like to hunt," he continued. "I've never done it before and I've always been curious. It felt like an itch that needed scratching."

I couldn't believe what I was hearing, that Bertram was going to take the fall for his son.

"Why the tiger, though? You know it was my favorite," Dad said, his face red with anger.

"I know. So, after I got this idea in my head, I went and retrieved one of the guns from the hunting lodge and went to the reserve. I was going to kill something easy, like one of the servals. But then, I got up there and the tiger was awake and I decided it was the one. Something came over me. So I shot him, three times, one after another, and immediately after, I knew it was a huge mistake. Killing the tiger sobered me up right away," he said.

"Yes, hunting is not a drunk man's sport," my dad agreed.

"I knew I'd be in huge trouble so I quickly ran to the security bank and scrambled all the footage so I wouldn't be found out. It was a rash, stupid decision but it was the only thing I could think to do in the moment."

I sat silent, but dumbfounded, listening to everything. My dad was quiet, taking it all in. He looked pissed, but let Bertram tell his whole story. When he was done, suddenly my dad started laughing, harder and harder, until Bertram nervously laughed along as well, and I did too.

"You're one crazy son of a bitch," my dad said, laughing as tears streamed down his face. "I always knew that, but somehow I always forgive you, don't I?"

"Yes, Gareth, that's right. So you forgive me now? I'm so sorry," Bertram said, sounding genuinely contrite. I almost believed him, if it wasn't for being the root of the truth.

"Yes, I forgive you," my dad said, and Bertram looked relieved. We were almost out of the woods. "But, I want to know one more thing," my dad asked, peering at Bertram with a curious look on his face.

"Anything you want to know Gareth, of course."

"How did it feel to kill something? Did it live up to the expectations you had built up in your mind? It's been so long since my first kill, I don't even remember what that is like, I'm afraid."

"It was amazing," Bertram said, feeding into what my dad wanted to hear.

"Good. So it was worth it?"

"Yes, I believe it was, although I'm embarrassed I did this behind your back. I should've just asked," he continued.

"Yes, you should've, but I forgive you. I know it's hard for you to ask me for things," my dad said. "One last item to discuss—"

"Yes?" Bertram asked.

"I'm going to need to punish you—publicly—in front of the White Suits. The word is out that someone killed the tiger and I need to show everyone that type of behavior is not tolerated here."

"I know," Bertram said. "I expect nothing less."

"So, tomorrow, we're going to take you out to the Coliseum and I'm going to let the Suits throw stones at you for three minutes, okay?" he asked, as if Bertram had any say in the discussion. "One minute for each bullet. I've already selected the strongest Suits with the best aim to participate, just to make sure you learn your lesson."

Bertram grimaced and I couldn't believe my dad could be so awful.

"Dad. That seems too harsh," I said, feeling terrible for Bertram, and for our stupidity to get him into this situation to begin with.

"I know, love, but this is what I have to do to keep people in line. Otherwise, we could have a sort of anarchy here."

"It's okay, Chelsea," Bertram said. "I must live with the consequences of my incredibly foolish actions," he continued, and I knew he was speaking to me about what Odin and I did.

"And, if Odin is well enough, I expect him to come watch too," my dad said. "No one is exempt from witnessing the punishments."

"Okay, understood," Bertram said, but looked grim.

"Well, I feel much better that we got to the bottom of things," my dad said. "Now, I need to go take a bath. You two are excused."

Bertram and I got up and left my dad's living quarters and walked down the hall together.

"You are *not* to say anything to Odin about this," Bertram instructed me. "He needs to recover and this will make him too upset," he said. I knew that was true. "I can't stand the thought of him seeing me tomorrow at the stoning, so he can't know until what's done is done," he said.

"Yes, okay," I agreed.

We parted ways and I spent the rest of the day feeling miserable. I couldn't see Odin and I was sick to my stomach thinking about what Bertram had to face tomorrow.

I went to find Elise. She was in her room looking at scientific drawings of animals on her computer.

"How is Odin doing?"

"He's in pain, but he's okay. He misses you," she said and that cheered me up slightly. "It will take him a few more days to recover enough to be back out again."

"Did you hear about Bertram?" I asked, feeling terrible that we were at fault.

"Yes, I did. He's a good man," she said. "He always has been," she said, looking sad. "He'll be okay, but you should take this as a very important lesson. Gareth doesn't mess around and will severely punish his closest friends, even his family, if he feels like his trust has been compromised."

"Is there anything we can do to get him to change his mind? And to stop tomorrow's beating?" I asked.

"Well, I've never been able to get Gareth to change his mind about anything. Once he decides something, it's his way or nothing. And he was absolutely furious about the tiger. He loved that damn thing."

I knew she was right. I went to bed with a heavy heart thinking about Odin and not knowing what was happening.

The next morning, my dad called me into his quarters very early, and no one else was there.

He looked at me sternly. "I know it was you and Odin who killed the tiger."

"What? I don't . . . "

"Stop, Chelsea. I've been close to Bertram for a very, very long time and I'm confident he'd do anything to protect his son. And when no one let me talk to Odin and the security footage was altered, I knew the truth right away. But, I wanted to see if *you'd* tell me the truth."

I felt sheepish and my face became hot with embarrassment.

"So it was disappointing to see you sit there and not say anything yesterday when Bertram pretended he did it. That man doesn't have a violent bone in his body. Even a drunk Bertram wouldn't have done that to the tiger. And you sat there and let him take the fall."

"I'm so sorry, Dad," I said, the truth spilling out of me. "I didn't know what to do. I was scared you'd hurt Odin."

"You really like him, don't you, Chelsea?" he asked, looking at me with that knowing gaze.

"Yes, Dad. He's my best friend in the whole world."

I didn't want him to know we had kissed.

"Well, it's a shame that you didn't speak up yesterday. I would've forgiven both of you, if you had just been honest. That's what matters most to me."

"I'm so sorry, Dad."

"Now I have to punish Bertram. I have no choice. It's how I keep the whole island in line. And you're going to come watch it happen. But first, take off your shirt."

"What? Why?" I said, my face feeling red hot at the suggestion. He pulled out a short, shiny stick.

"I'm going to strike you for every bullet, too. But I'm going to hit your back, so no one else sees the marks it'll leave behind. This punishment is just between me and you," he continued. I felt terrified but knew I couldn't get away. I peeled off my shirt and stood in my bra before him, feeling my face burn in shame.

"Turn around," he ordered.

I slowly pivoted to face away from him. Without a warning, he struck me sharply in the middle of my back and I screamed out in pain, louder with each strike. The pain was agonizing and I struggled to remain standing.

"Good girl," he said. "Now get ready—it's time for us to go outside."

After I put my shirt back on, he led me by the hand out the door, down the hall, and into the blinding sun of the Coliseum floor.

Bertram was there, tied up to a post, and he looked at us sadly.

"It's a beautiful day for a beating, huh?" he called up, joking.

My dad chuckled and we sat there waiting, as the White Suits began to file in to start the day's proceedings.

CHAPTER 18

Chelsea — Age 14

O din and I spent every day running around the island and heading to our favorite private spots to fool around.

One morning, we went out early and we ran up the hill toward a cave that was tucked in the mountainside that overlooked the island and the ocean.

We looked down from the top, as we always did because it was such an incredible view, and in the distance we saw a new boat approaching. It wasn't one of the mega yachts that brought the Praeclarus members, but a simpler sailboat.

It came toward the dock slowly and I pulled out my binoculars to get a better look.

After White Suits tied up the boat, people started getting off. They looked to be handcuffed, but I couldn't be sure.

"What is it?" Odin asked, as he couldn't see. I handed him the binoculars and he strained to figure out what was going on. "I think those are kids around our age," he said, confused.

It reminded me of when Bertram and Odin arrived years ago, and I wondered if my dad had brought more people for us to hang out with. I knew in my heart that this wasn't the explanation, but I couldn't think of anything else it could be.

When new Suits arrived, they walked on their own free will—not handcuffed—and were cleaner than this group that looked to be in ragged clothing, and dirty.

"Let's go see what this is about," I said, and we both ran down the hill quickly, eager to get to the

bottom of the mystery. As we were sprinting down the path, we ran into Elise.

"Where are you two lovebirds going so quickly this morning?" she asked.

She was one of the few people on the island that knew about our relationship. She actually supported it and acted happy for me. In fact, one day she handed me a little book of pills and told me to take one every day to make sure I didn't have a baby. I didn't want a baby so I was thankful for her help.

"A new boat just arrived, and it looks like a bunch of kids just got off of it," I explained. "But we couldn't tell for sure, so we're going to get a closer look."

"Kids? What do you mean?" she asked, confused. "Like children?"

"No, like teenagers," Odin said. "People around our age."

Elise looked disturbed. "That's not good," she muttered under her breath.

"What's not good?" I asked, as we continued walking along the path toward the dock, Elise right behind us.

"Nothing. I'm afraid it's just Gareth upping the stakes," she said. I had no idea what she meant.

We got to the dock and saw that they were teenagers, but they all looked like they had seen better days. Elise ran up to a man that was standing with them.

"Ames? Is that you?" she asked, grabbing onto his arm and peering up at him.

"Elise! Hello! Are you part of the welcoming committee?" he joked and hugged her. It seemed like they were old friends.

"What are you doing here?" she asked. "And who are these kids?" she continued, pointing to the group of kids, who all appeared exhausted.

"Gareth's hired me to help whip them into shape. It's like a rehab program," he explained. "For troubled kids. They're from all over the world, and we're their last hope. He told me it would be a humanitarian mission, and he offered to pay me handsomely, so here I am."

Elise's brow was furrowed like she was thinking through something carefully, and I wondered what was going on. I counted ten kids in total. Suddenly, my dad strode down the dock and brushed past Elise, giving Ames a long hug.

"Hello, old friend. Thank you for coming. We need your expertise badly," my dad said.

Ames smiled. He was quite muscular. He was the most fit person I'd ever seen. Odin and I sat and watched, confused as to what was really happening.

"Well, let's take them to their quarters, shall we? Let's allow them to rest today and we'll start 'em on the program tomorrow."

"What program?" I asked. My dad looked back at me with an annoyed expression.

"That is none of your business, Chelsea. Now you and Odin go off and mind yourselves," he ordered, and we had to listen to him. As we left, we turned back, trying to figure out what was happening.

"He's such an asshole," Odin muttered.

I felt a twinge of confusion because he was right, my dad was frequently terrible, but he was *my* dad. I didn't like when somebody said something bad about him, even Odin.

Odin hated my dad ever since he found out about my punishment and Bertram's stoning after the tiger incident. It was a secret that couldn't be kept from him because he saw the bruised lines along my back, and Bertram was black and blue in the face for a good week after the beating. Everyone talked about it for some time. It was the most exciting thing that had happened on the island for a while.

"I know where they are being taken," I said suddenly as we walked up the path. "They're being taken to that new building, the one we can't go in," I said.

The workers had built a new structure and forum area next to the Coliseum, but no one told us what it was for. Every time we tried to sneak a peek inside, we were shooed away—Dad's orders.

It drove us crazy trying to figure out what the building was going to be used for and we speculated all sort of crazy ideas, but none of them involved a bunch of kids coming to the island. I wondered where they were from specifically, and if they spoke English. It sounded like they were troubled kids, and I felt hopeful that maybe my dad was entering a new, softer stage where he wanted to help others.

Odin and I ran up the hill again and took turns using the binoculars to watch the group as they trudged slowly toward the structure. I was right. But why were they here?

CHAPTER 19

Gareth – 2 years ago

"Hear me out, my brother, hear me out," I said to Bertram. He wasn't listening to me and he was starting to make me angry.

We had been drinking in the game room for hours and discussing the future of the island. He was excited about the prospect of the hybrid animals' development thus far—and my even wilder plans—but we were still a few years away from any of it being ready to share with all of Praeclarus.

I needed something else new to excite the Praeclarus guys. I felt their interest waning a bit on recent trips. They were bored with all the activities I offered—the sex, the drinking, and the hunting were growing stale. I sensed that I was losing the enthusiasm of the crowd and knew I needed to mix things up. I was their leader and it was my responsibility.

My long-percolating ideas were reinforced when I saw how excited people were when Louis was made to fight Eche, and the other Suit fights. That was intriguing, but what if I upped the stakes and helped rid cities of future criminals?

"Kids? You can't be serious?" Bertram argued.

"Not normal kids. Low-lifes, drifters, druggies, and criminals. I'm doing their communities a favor by getting rid of them before they have time to create real damage. It's like a community service."

Bertram just sighed like he was disgusted.

"Where are you going to get them from? What about their families?"

"I'll cherry-pick them using my scouts to make

sure that only kids that are runaways or estranged from their families get taken away. I don't want to draw unnecessary attention to their disappearances, after all."

"But why kids?"

"Because they're beautiful. And they're so wide-eyed and hopeful—even the losers can be cleaned up and primed for fighting. Have you seen the way Praeclarus members look at Chelsea and Odin? They're envious of their looks, of their youth. It's one of the only things their money can't buy. I think they'll enjoy seeing young kids battling it out—it's like our own little Hollywood production, but live in the flesh. You want good-looking actors, right?"

"I think you're losing it, Gareth," Bertram said, his words beginning to slur. "I believe this island and Praeclarus are making you go insane. Honestly. That's what I think."

He had never talked to me like this and I felt myself getting angry that he wasn't getting it, that he didn't share my vision for what this island could become.

"Be careful, Bertram," I warned, and I meant it. I didn't like him questioning me. It was like my closest allies were turning against me. First Elise, then Bertram. "Remember what I saved you from?" I asked him.

Before I came to the island, I had heard that Bertram was in crippling debt and that people were out to kill him. And I, out of the goodness of my heart, reached out and saved him.

It would be a symbiotic relationship—as all of my relationships were—as he had a skill set developing complex security systems that I could use here on the island. It was funny—this expert in security was afraid for his own life. When I reached out, he agreed rather quickly to the plan to move to the island for good, as long as his young son Odin could come along. He feared for his boy's safety as well.

I told him not to drag the kid into this but the

bastard brought him anyway. That boy had been a pain in my ass practically since arriving, taking Chelsea away and encouraging her to participate in all sorts of mischief. I knew she had a crush on him and that her allegiance to me was starting to weaken.

"I do remember what you saved me from," Bertram responded, and he shoved his drink down forcefully. He was getting sloppy drunk, which I hated. It was so uncouth. "You saved me from evil. And now look what you've become," he said.

"You're calling me evil?"

"Yes, I am. Listen to yourself. You're not the same man I became friends with so many years ago."

Now he was starting to sound like Elise, and that really pissed me off. Bertram continued, "You're talking about putting children into the Coliseum to fight one another to the death."

"They're not children. They're practically adults, the ones I'm interested in. And, while they're here, I'll treat them well. I'll put them in nice living quarters and sober them up and fatten them up and train them to fight so they'll make for the best show possible. I have just the person to help me with that, actually."

"You've really lost it. If you go through with this plan, I'll make sure you don't get away with it," Bertram said.

"Are you threatening me?"

"Yes, I think I am," Bertram said, and burped a laugh to himself. "I know things about the island's security system that you don't. I can expose what's going on here to the public—easy."

"You better watch yourself, Bertram," I said, not liking the ugly turn this conversation had taken. He'd always been a terrible drunk, but in every drunk person's words, there was an ounce of truth and I was very disturbed by what he was saying.

"I think it's time you go to bed, Bertram."

I took him by the arm and firmly led him to his room where he collapsed onto his bed.

The next morning, he apologized profusely and begged for my forgiveness, saying that he'd support me no matter what my plans were for the island. I hugged him back, and assured him everything was okay.

But, I knew what I needed to do. He had become too much of a liability. The day after the first group of kids came to the island, I went into Bertram's room while he was still sleeping.

"There's an issue at the hangar, Bertram. Wake up!"

"Huh? What?" he opened his eyes, looking totally confused.

"The cages opened. We need to go fix it right now."

"But I'm still drunk," he said, kind of laughing to himself.

"This is an emergency, so get up, now." I pulled him out of bed and we stumbled down the long pathway leading to the hangar, past Wexler who gave me a look and then went back to watching his TV screen.

I opened the hangar and we went inside. I turned on the lights. The animals were all sick and not right yet. We were not ready to debut them, which made me feel anxious.

"Do you remember what we argued about that night a few weeks ago, when you were wasted?" I asked Bertram, who looked at me, confused.

"About the animals? Or the security system? Everything looks okay here to me," he said, glancing around the room, confused. All the cages were closed. He didn't remember the specifics of the argument, just thought we had fought.

I pulled out my gun from my belt and aimed it at him.

He suddenly looked alert and confused. "Wait . . . what are you doing?"

"I'm sorry, my friend," I said, and I was genuinely sorry as I pulled the trigger, shooting him in the forehead. He crumpled to the ground. As his arms twisted unnaturally underneath him, a pool of blood quickly spread under his head. Whenever I had to kill someone, it always surprised me that it didn't feel all that different from killing one of the animals in the game area.

I was sorry that in his drunken state, he revealed what he *truly* felt. He didn't share my vision for the island. I thought we'd live here into our old age together and see all of our hard work and accomplishments come to life.

I had to get rid of him, though. He knew too much and I feared that he'd expose the island's secrets. That couldn't happen—not to me; not to my dear Chelsea; and not to all the Praeclarus members who trusted me with their secret proclivities.

I left the hangar and told Wexler that he'd have to clean up in there. He saw that I was alone.

"Yes sir, whatever you say." He nodded at me.

He was one of my most loyal Suits, and I took extra special care of him.

I went back to my room and thought about what to tell everyone about Bertram's whereabouts. Thankfully, everyone knew he was a heavy drinker, so it seemed pretty easy.

I went and found Odin and Chelsea as they ate breakfast next to each other. They thought I didn't catch them holding hands, but what was going on between them was clear as day.

"I wanted to tell you first before you heard from everyone else. Bertram is missing. He was drinking hard last night and the last time anyone saw him was at the dock," I said, doing my best to look alarmed.

"What?" Chelsea got up.

"What do you mean?" Odin cried out.

"Your father is missing. I've sent out a search crew but no one has been able to locate him. I'm afraid he might've fallen into the water."

"No, that's impossible," Odin said. "My dad

hates the water. He wouldn't have gone near the dock."

"He was very drunk last night," I told him. "People do all sort of stupid things when they've had too much."

"No, it can't be true. He must be sleeping it off somewhere. I'll go find him."

"I'm going with you," Chelsea insisted.

They ran off, Odin looking serious but scared, and Chelsea following close behind. They knew every corner and hiding place on the island, except the hangar where they weren't allowed.

They spent the next couple of days searching every single spot, using that map that they drew years ago to make sure they didn't forget any nook or cranny. Their dedication was kind of sweet, but I knew they wouldn't find anything. Wexler had taken care of it.

We reviewed the tapes, and nothing suspicious was found, because I made sure of it. After a week, the search was called off.

Odin wasn't the same after that. He withdrew and seemed angry whenever we'd cross paths. No one else seemed any the wiser, but somehow, it felt like Odin knew the truth.

I'd smile at him and ask him how he was holding up, but he always remained silent, refusing to talk to me.

I was starting to really hate that little shit, and didn't like the fact that he was taking Chelsea away from me all the time. Sometimes it felt like she didn't even like me very much.

Frustrated that Bertram and Elise had turned against me, I felt like I had to take action to improve the island so I'd keep the Praeclarus members under my thumb.

Now that I had a group of kids on the island, it was time to enact the next stage of the plan. I reached out to Ames and he was game to come here to help me. In fact, he recruited the first set of kids, and when I greeted them at the dock on their arrival day and looked them over, I knew they'd work out just fine.

Sure, they were dirty and mangy and strung out, but their bones were good, they were young and handsome, and they could be built up and trained quickly.

I was excited to show off this new activity to the Praeclarus club, when the time was right. This first batch took many months to train, and Ames thought it was just part of a plan to get them clean. He loved it—it was his new life purpose.

When it was time for the first match, I put the two best-looking, strongest boys against each other. I made sure Chelsea, Odin, and all the unnecessary Suits were kept away, as I wanted the first fight to be an intimate affair to share with just my friends. The Praeclarus members asked many questions about what was happening. A few were upset and vocal about it—but I reminded them this was getting rid of kids that wouldn't amount to much—and that their lives were better spent and lost here than becoming criminals at home. I showed them dossiers on each kid, and the crimes they'd committed in their home cities—at such a young age. Sharing that information seemed to make everything a little bit more palatable, and eventually, as I expected, the Praeclarus members began to like the fights. Their cheering became heartier, the bets flowed freely, and the sport was born just as I envisioned it.

But Ames, no matter what I said to try to sway him, didn't like the truth about why we were training kids. He didn't have much of a choice, though; I made that clear. The trip to the island was one way, and there was no turning back. As long as he took care of the kids, I'd take care of him. He knew that I meant it, so he took his job seriously—he wanted to live. He was amazing at sculpting the kids into talented fighters and ready-ing them for battle.

The whole thing worked so well; I was amazed that it took me so long to make the plan a reality.

I couldn't wait until the Creatures were ready—
that would be really something.

CHAPTER 20

In the Coliseum, the Komodo dragon-tiger creature was angry and it hissed loudly, causing everyone to cheer as it started to run toward Reed, who tried to lunge out of the way. The lizard mouth grabbed his leg and flung him to the ground immediately.

Reed screamed out in pain and kicked hard, trying to free himself from the Creature's grip. The Creature clamped its claws around Reed's thigh and shook him.

Reed took his dagger and swung it toward the lizard face, plunging it into its cheek and causing the animal to release its grip momentarily. He got up and ran as fast as he could away from the Creature, looking around for anything to use as another weapon.

He reached down and grabbed two large rocks on the ground. When the animal recovered, it hissed even louder and ran back toward Reed, who flung the rocks. One of them hit the animal in its head, which only momentarily stunned it before it charged Reed again.

My dad cheered next to me. Instead of joining in like I usually did, I felt completely helpless and frustrated that there was nothing I could do to help.

When the Creature reached Reed again, it took Reed down to the ground by his left arm and tore his shoulder open.

Just then, Delphine darted up and before anyone could stop her, she jumped over the wall, dropping fifteen feet. She reached down and grabbed the dagger that was laying bloody on the ground, her long purple dress whipping behind her.

My dad got up and yelled, "Stop her!" to the

White Suit standing next to him. The man hesitated then jumped down as well, but it was too late, as Delphine was already at the Creature, who was ripping at Reed's arm and shoulder angrily.

Delphine screamed out as she plunged the knife into the animal's fur-covered neck. The Creature shrieked and let go of Reed. It toppled backward, and Delphine stabbed it in the back, causing it to stumble and turn angrily toward her.

Reed was bloodied and crippled, but somehow managed to step up and grab at the animal's tail. He yanked it hard, causing the Creature to whip around and become confused momentarily. Delphine let out another savage scream and lunged forward with the dagger, swinging her arm around to slit the animal's throat. It still moved, trying to grab at Delphine with its claws. She moved away and stabbed it one more time in the back, causing blood to spew out of its mouth until it became still.

Delphine ran over to Reed and collapsed next to him. She lifted him up and cradled him in her arms. He was bleeding heavily and I wondered if he would make it out alive. Was the Komodo's bite truly poisonous? I glanced back at Ames, who was staring down at the Coliseum floor, his mouth open.

"Someone go help him, now!" Ames said. My dad looked back and glared at him.

Before anyone could say another word, the White Suits were out there with the stretcher. One pushed Delphine away and tossed Reed on the stretcher. One of them quickly plunged a giant syringe into his chest, and then they took him through the gate.

I knew they were taking him to Elise, and I hoped she had the capability to save him. From the puddle of blood on the ground and all over Delphine, it was obvious he had lost a ton.

The crowd was standing and cheering wildly. My dad looked thrilled, taking it all in. He didn't seem all that upset that Delphine had left his side, as she really just added to the show.

She was on the ground, covered in Reed's blood, with the skirt of her dress gathered around her like a purple blossom. The camera zoomed into her face as she sobbed loudly. It was the first time I'd seen her cry.

My dad just sat there taking in all the glory of his friends cheering him on. And for some reason, something clicked in my head. I had had enough.

As everyone around me celebrated, I stood up and jumped over the wall too. I fell hard on the ground, scraping my legs. My dad didn't seem to notice at first. I popped up and ran toward Delphine as fast as I could. I suddenly heard him yelling after me.

"Chelsea! What are you doing?" he screamed. I just didn't care anymore. The people in the crowd howled and heckled me, and I felt so small down there.

"This must stop! My dad is a criminal! And so are all of you!" I screamed. As I ran toward her, Delphine looked up, surprised. She sort of got up halfway, like I was going to attack her, but that wasn't it at all.

I reached her, collapsed next to her, and held her close in my arms.

The crowd went crazy, like it was some sort of staged lesbian scene.

Delphine cried out to me, "What are you doing?"

I pulled her head in close and whispered, "Let's get out here."

I wasn't sure how we were going to do it, but I suddenly felt like I *had* to trust Elise and Ames. My dad hadn't kept one promise, and I realized I was going to die here if I didn't fight back.

I wanted to see what the real world was like. I didn't care about the gifts and jewelry and material things that my dad gave me.

"Chelsea, come back here right now!" My dad screamed. "Have you lost your mind? Someone go get her! Put her in lockdown!"

And suddenly, I felt someone's arms around

me, pulling me off of Delphine, lifting me up into the air and into their arms. I kicked and screamed and tried to get away, but it was no use.

I knew where I was heading. They were taking me to the confinement room and I had no idea when I'd see freedom again. I looked back and saw Delphine staring at me, her mouth open, yelling something I couldn't hear.

CHAPTER 21

Chelsea – Age 14

We tried to figure out what was going on with the new kids, but no one would tell us exactly what was happening.

One night, Odin came to me while I was sleeping. He knew the code to my room, but rarely used it for fear of getting caught. So, when he came in, I knew immediately that something was wrong.

"I found something in my room I want to show you," he said.

I was still half asleep and totally confused. "What are you talking about?"

I could barely see him, so I turned on my bed-side light. He seemed like he had been crying.

"Look at this," he said, handing me a piece of paper. It was a letter.

"What is this?"

"It's from my dad," he said, starting to sob.

"What? Where did you get it?"

"It was under my mattress in my bed frame. When I went to grab an apple that rolled under my bed, I saw something sticking out from under the frame. I'd never looked under the bed before, so it surprised me."

I opened the letter and looked at it, trying to figure out if it was real. But why would it be fake?

The date was a week before Bertram went missing.

I read it quickly.

Dearest Odin—

My good, good boy. I'm sorry to have gotten you into this mess. When I accepted the offer to come here, I thought our world would get better, and instead, I fear what this place is becoming.

If I'm not here one day, please know it's because I spoke up against what I believe is wrong. That's all I've ever known. And I hope you, my boy, will follow in my footsteps and fight against the injustices you see here.

I know nothing for sure, except this island is getting worse by the day and I don't know how much longer I can take it.

You're a stronger boy than I am a man.

Be true to yourself.

—Bertram

I looked up at Odin, who was full-on sobbing again.

"Is this real?"

"Yes, of course," he sounded angry that I was questioning it. I was just in disbelief.

"What do you think this means? Did he commit suicide?" I wondered out loud.

"No! It means that he was murdered!" Odin said, like it was as clear as day.

"How do you get that . . . from this?" I asked. The letter was threatening, but not outright saying he feared for his life or anything. "Murdered? That is crazy. Who would murder him?"

"Jesus, are you dense? Gareth! Your dad would do that! You know it in your heart."

I didn't know what to think. I couldn't believe that my dad would kill anyone, let alone Bertram, who was his closet and oldest friend and ally.

"I have to go see him," Odin said, with that angry look in his eye that scared me. I had seen it a few times and I knew he couldn't be easily talked down.

"No, you can't do that. You've got to think this through. You can't be sure that's what the letter is saying, and my dad won't like the accusation."

"Are you not on my side?"

"Of course I'm on your side!" I cried out. "I just don't want to see you hurt. I love you!"

"Then come with me to talk to Gareth," he said, looking at me desperately. I felt uncomfortable taking sides and thought it was really unfair of him to put that on me. I loved my dad, despite his huge, obvious flaws.

I didn't respond and he looked at me in disbelief. "Fine!" He turned and ran out, slamming the door behind him. As soon as he left, I collapsed on the bed and cried, totally clueless about what to do.

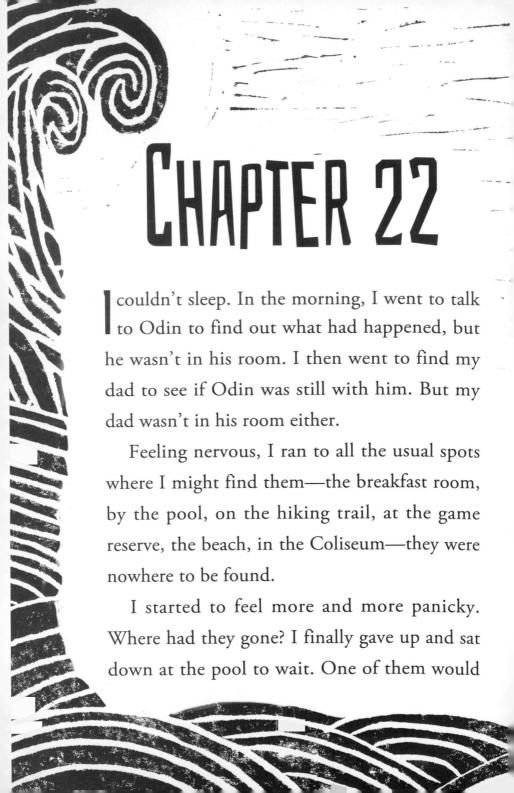

CHAPTER 22

I couldn't sleep. In the morning, I went to talk to Odin to find out what had happened, but he wasn't in his room. I then went to find my dad to see if Odin was still with him. But my dad wasn't in his room either.

Feeling nervous, I ran to all the usual spots where I might find them—the breakfast room, by the pool, on the hiking trail, at the game reserve, the beach, in the Coliseum—they were nowhere to be found.

I started to feel more and more panicky. Where had they gone? I finally gave up and sat down at the pool to wait. One of them would come find me here; I knew it. I just had to be patient, which was the worst thing.

Finally, my dad appeared, looking down at me, concerned. "Sweetie, I need to talk to you about something."

That didn't sound good. "Where's Odin?" I demanded, standing up to face him angrily.

"Did you know about him coming to see me?" he asked, searching my face.

"Yes, he thought you murdered Bertram," I said

"Yes, that's what he said, before he tried to kill me," he responded, turning his cheek to show large scratches across his face.

"He did that?"

I didn't believe that Odin would assault him.

"Yes, that little shit almost succeeded, too, but thankfully Ames heard me screaming and tore him off of me."

"Oh my God," I sighed, collapsing to the ground. I couldn't believe what I was hearing and

knew it wasn't good for Odin. This was what I had been afraid of.

"So, is he going to have to face a beating tomorrow? Please don't hurt him," I begged, knowing that Odin had acted rashly and didn't think things through. I hated the idea of him being stoned, and made an example of to all the Suits.

"Not quite, my love. I can't trust him being out and about any longer."

"What? What do you mean?" I demanded.

"I've moved him to the training area."

"Wait . . . what's that?" I cried, reaching over to grab his arm so he'd look at me. "You mean, where the other kids live?"

"Yes, that's it exactly. He'll make some new friends over there. I need you to stay away from him. He'll quickly realize what a huge mistake he made challenging me."

"Dad! I can't do that. He's my only friend

in this whole wide world." I started to cry, not believing my dad was being so cruel.

"What happens at training? I still don't understand."

"You'll see, my dear. Ames thinks Odin shows a lot of promise. He's very brave—if not a little dumb and impulsive—but he is special."

"What do you mean?"

"Chelsea—I need you to remember one thing, and one thing only in the coming weeks."

"Yes, Dad?" I said, in between sniffled cries.

"I love you more than anything in the entire world, and I'll do anything to protect you and to protect me. Anything. Odin tried to kill me, Chelsea. Just whatever happens in the future, please remember that, okay? He was going to take me away from you."

He patted me on the head and then kissed my cheek, which was wet from tears.

I had told Odin to stay away and now we were

forced apart. I hated my dad for separating us, and I hated Odin for being so stupid.

CHAPTER 23

The first time Odin faced a fight, I couldn't believe it. My dad warned me to stay away that day, but I needed to know what was happening, so I went to the Coliseum and sat far away from everyone else, not wanting to talk to anyone. I had a bad feeling in my gut and I needed to see it.

I hadn't seen Odin since that night he confronted my dad. I tried to go to the training area, but the Suits wouldn't let me in—my dad's orders. It was unusual for them to refuse me, but they wouldn't budge.

So, the day of the first fight, I didn't know what was happening, exactly, and I was shocked to see Odin walk out of the gate, half-naked, with another boy right behind him. When my dad ordered them to fight, I couldn't believe it and I ran over to my dad, telling him to make it stop, but he wouldn't. He looked around at the crowd, who were cheering at Odin and the boy to attack each other. Odin and the other kid both refused, looking bewildered by their surroundings. Suits with arrows suddenly appeared and my dad threatened them to begin fighting, or they'd be killed outright in a single shot.

To my horror, Odin and the boy ran toward the center and began beating each other. Odin was winning. He was so very strong and he kept going, hitting the kid again and again until the boy went limp beneath him.

I couldn't believe my sweet, serious Odin just punched another kid to death. What was happening?

When he finished, he looked stunned, his face and hands splattered with blood. He saw me and I ran down to the edge. He hobbled over in obvious pain and reached up, but the wall was much too tall. Suits came and pulled him away, removing him from the Coliseum floor.

That night, I went into my dad's room, confronting him.

"Wait. Before you say anything, remember when I said I'd do anything to protect you?" he asked as I was sobbing. I shook my head.

How could he be so cruel?

He continued, "Odin is dangerous, Chelsea. He thinks I killed Bertram. That boy loved his father so much, he'll now do whatever he can to avenge a wrong that I didn't commit," he said.

I felt confused.

"And I'm afraid he may hurt you just to get at me."

"Odin would never hurt me!" I said, knowing that it was true. We loved each other. Odin just made a dumb mistake in haste when he was upset. He didn't really want to kill my dad. "And, he didn't mean to hurt you," I pleaded. "Just give him a shot to talk to you and make things right."

"We'll see, my dear," my dad said, pulling me in for a hug. "But I think there is one thing we can both agree on," he continued, dabbing at my tears with a handkerchief.

"What's that?"

"That Odin is quite a good fighter, isn't he?"

I nodded, and had a horrible feeling in my stomach that Odin and I would not be reunited any time soon.